STEELE

SHADOWRIDGE GUARDIANS MC

PEPPER NORTH

PHOTOGRAPHY BY
FURIOUSFOTOG/GOLDENCZERMAK

COVER MODEL
DYLAN HORSCH

Pepper North
With a Wink Publishing, LLC

Text copyright© 2023 Pepper North
All Rights Reserved

ABOUT SHADOWRIDGE GUARDIANS MC

Combining the sizzling talents of bestselling authors Pepper North, Kate Oliver, and Becca Jameson, the Shadowridge Guardians are guaranteed to give you a thrill and leave you dreaming of your own throbbing motorcycle joyride.

Are you daring enough to ride with a club of rough, growly, commanding men? The protective Daddies of the Shadowridge Guardians Motorcycle Club will stop at nothing to ensure the safety and protection of everything that belongs to them: their Littles, their club, and their town. Throw in some sassy, naughty, mischievous women who won't hesitate to serve their fair share of attitude even in the face of looming danger, and this brand new MC Romance series is ready to ignite!

Shadowridge Guardians MC
Steele
Kade
Atlas
Doc
Gabriel

Talon
Bear
Faust
Storm

CHAPTER ONE

Cursing her desire to finish the last details on her clandestine report, Ivy carefully stowed the printed page in the desk and grabbed her purse and coat to leave. She was still trying to prove to the bank president that he hadn't made a mistake in hiring a twenty-eight-year-old as the bank manager. The interior of the building was eerily quiet with only a few lights on inside as she walked to the back door. Cautiously, she looked out the security peephole before dashing outside and pushing the door closed behind her.

They were on her before she stepped forward. Two, maybe three men slammed her against the bricks before grabbing her arms behind her back. A scream burst from her lips and echoed against the surrounding buildings. One powerful hand held her head restrained from looking at them with a painful yank on her ponytail.

Tears burst into her eyes, and Ivy tried to blink them away. "You're on security cam. I don't know what you mean to do, but facial recognition will have you identified in a flash. Let me go and I won't say a thing."

"Right..." One deep voice drew out that word sarcastically.

Damn, that didn't work. Would her scream bring anyone? She could hear faint wisps of music from The Hangout, about three blocks away.

"You're going to tell us the bank codes to get in and then you'll walk us inside to collect access to a few accounts for us," another voice informed her with clipped military precision.

"The bank is on a time lock. Once the last person leaves, it won't open until tomorrow morning when the bank opens," she told them quickly, making up an excuse to keep them from forcing her back into bank.

"And I'm sure, Ms. Bank Manager, you have the skills to override that."

"I don't. I'm just the manager. I do the paperwork. The bank president can do that, but not me," she rushed to correct them.

"Tell us the door code and we'll just wander around inside to see what we find," the first voice instructed.

"I can't do that. I'll lose my job," she protested. The yank to her hair informed her they didn't care. "Besides, I just changed the code. I don't remember it."

Another vicious jerk on her ponytail brought more tears to her eyes. "I think it's time to teach this bitch a lesson. We have just become your worst nightmare. You're going to work for us, Ms. Bank Manager, from now on. That is, if you survive this lesson of what we're capable of."

Strong hands jerked her wrists harder behind her and tied them tightly with a rope. She bit her lip as the rough fibers bit into her skin. A ripping sound came from behind her, and a large hand reached in front of her to slap a piece of duct tape over her mouth. Her heart felt like it would beat out of her chest.

She panicked as rough fabric draped over her face. Thrashing her body from side to side, Ivy felt her hair tearing from her scalp. Scared beyond thought, she wet herself.

"Get her legs tied."

They lifted Ivy effortlessly, flipping her horizontally and lowering her to the cement. She landed with a thud, and the air flooded out of her nostrils when they dropped her several inches. While she recovered her breath, they stripped her shoes off and bound her feet close to her hands.

"Pissed all over herself," one guy said, sounding divided between pride and disdain as he finished pulling the bag around her body.

When it pulled together below her knees, Ivy knew they'd knotted the burlap around her. She prayed as they lifted her and dropped her into the back of a vehicle with a thud. The door slamming down felt like her coffin closing.

Pushing back his chair, Steele rose to his feet. "I'm headed back to the compound. Anyone else ready to leave?"

Just as he thought, his MC brothers refused his invitation to ride back together. They were having way too much fun at The Hangout, Shadowridge's local roadhouse. The establishment was always good for a round of drinks when they showed up. Having the motorcycle club roll up added an edgy feel to the place that made everyone thirsty.

And the twenty-somethings? They loved flirting with the guys they considered the ultimate bad boys in town.

Steele shook his head at the girls already ensconced on a few laps. No wonder no one was ready to go.

"Hey. You're not leaving, are you?" a cute blonde asked, daringly tracing the black tattoo on his forearm.

"Yes."

"You… You could stay for a while. Maybe dance with me?" She stuttered at first but gained confidence as she spoke.

"Not this time."

Turning, he heard Talon call, "I'm a much better dancer, baby," to tempt the blonde to change her target.

Without changing his trajectory, Steele flipped the smartass off and exited with the laughter of his motorcycle brethren following him out. He headed around the side of the building to where they had reserved parking. The raucous music from The Hangout wasn't quite as loud back here.

He scowled at the sight of two men standing way too close to the bikes. Approaching, Steele said, "Can I do something for you?"

"Just admiring the bikes. I like riding too. How do I get into the Shadowridge Guardians?" the older one asked.

"Invitation only. Go to our website and apply," he growled. The Guardians definitely weren't online.

A rhythmic banging sound caught his attention and Steele scanned the area, trying to zero in on its location. *There!* Steele stalked forward. It seemed to come from the dumpster.

"Hey, thanks. I'm Bill, by the way."

Ignoring the men he'd now dismissed as zero threats, Steele laid his hand on the metal dumpster and felt the vibration. *Damn it!* Someone had dropped an animal inside like they were trash.

Jumping to stand on the lower rim of the opening, he steadied himself from tumbling into the mess inside. Dark shadows hid in the corners as he studied the debris from the roadhouse slopped inside. A movement caught his eye, and he shifted forward, testing each step as he moved to the edge of the pile. One end of a burlap bag jerked, striking the metal wall of the dumpster.

Grabbing a hold of the material, Steele hauled it up through the muck that partially covered it. It was heavier than he expected. Not puppies, but definitely something alive. Maybe a big dog. It shook, obviously petrified by the sudden movement.

"It's okay, buddy. I've got you now. Hold still. I'll get us out of this before I track down the asshole who put you in here," Steele reassured the creature.

"Did you find something in there?"

Steele struggled to remember his name and gave up. "Come, take this so I won't hurt it getting out."

"There's something alive in there?"

"Here." Steele maneuvered the bundle out the entrance and fumed when the men stepped back from the filth coating it. Like they could be MC brothers. Bracing the sack on the opening, he jumped down and lowered it to the ground, unaided.

Holding the material away from the wiggling contents, Steele flicked his blade open and sliced through the top. A mass of dark hair popped into view. It was contained in a blue scrunchie. "Fuck!" This wasn't a dog. He sliced faster.

Realizing he needed some help, he swung the arm holding the knife around to point at the two men still gawking nearby. "You! Go find my guys. Tell them Bikes."

"That's all you want me to say?" the guy with what's-his-name asked.

"Bikes!" Steele roared at him and watched both men stumble back and race inside.

"It's okay, sweetheart. You can trust me. I'll get you out of here."

He watched her head continue to move to the side to bang against the metal of the dumpster. Steele knew her mind had checked out a while ago, but her survival instinct kept her doing the only thing she could to make noise. He freed her hands and feet from the rope that hogtied her. Wiping the filth off his hands on his shirt under his cut, Steele cradled her face. He ripped the duct tape quickly from her mouth, knowing a slow movement would just prolong the pain. She gasped for air as the Shadowridge Guardians flowed into the area.

"Call 911. We need an ambulance and the cops," Steele directed, running his free hand over her extremities to make sure nothing was broken. "Someone dumped her in the trash."

Kade dialed without asking any other questions. The grimace of anger on the Enforcer's face rivaled the other men as they pieced together what had happened. And the fate that had awaited her. The sanitation workers came early Sunday morning to dump the remains of the Saturday party crowd. The compactor would have crushed her.

Pushing those thoughts from his mind, Steele picked her up, cradling her against him. She was coated with leftover beer, cocktails, and the greasy bar food that The Hangout specialized in. It had seeped through the burlap bag, plastering the tailored suit to her body. A faint smell of urine clung to her, fueling his anger. They'd scared her into losing control.

"Here, Steele." The chaplain held a soft, stuffed bear close.

"Thanks, Gabriel." He tucked it into her arms. The stuffie didn't care if she wasn't clean.

As he watched, she lifted the bear to her face and buried her nose in the plush. Her banging movement ceased as she seemed to take comfort in the soft companion. He felt a tug on his vest and looked down to see her fingers gripping the edge of his cut. Steele hugged her against his chest. "It's going to be okay, Little girl. I promise. Can you tell me your name?"

Her eyelids opened for the first time, allowing him to see the brilliant green eyes they had hidden.

"Hey, Emerald Eyes. Can you tell me your name? I'm Steele."

This time, she seemed to focus on him, but didn't answer. Her gaze fastened on his face as if she were memorizing his features. He continued to talk to her as the police and ambulance pulled up.

"Here come the good guys. They're going to take care of you and find whoever did this to you."

"What's going on?" the senior patrolman asked, as he tried to size up the threatening crowd.

"I found her in the dumpster. She was bound and tied in that sack," Steele said, beckoning the medics forward.

"We'll take good care of her," one paramedic assured Steele as he reached forward to take the woman from his arms.

"Steele," she croaked, holding on to him with one hand locked like a death grip on his vest.

"Baby, they need to check you over. I know you've hurt your head." Steele talked to her quietly as the paramedics watched.

Almost immediately, her head banging started again. Steele cupped her jaw, preventing her from hitting herself against his chest. "It's okay, sweetheart."

"This is how I found her. I heard the noise of an impact against the metal sides of the dumpster. They'd hogtied and thrown her into the far corner. She was on automatic pilot, banging her head to make a racket. Who knows how long she was there," Steele explained.

"I think you need to come with her, sir. Would you put her on the gurney so we can assess her condition?" the female paramedic asked.

In an awkward position with her in his arms, he'd never be able to stand up without jarring her or putting his precious cargo down. "Boost me," he requested with a nod at the club members behind him. Bear and Talon moved forward to haul Steele to his feet. He thanked the burly guys for their help with a nod. Now standing, he carried the woman to the waiting stretcher and laid her on the crisp sheet. Her hand never loosened, and Steele wasn't about to pry himself loose.

"We need to take her to the hospital, sir. Perhaps you'd like to come with her?"

"Definitely."

Steele looked over his shoulder to throw his keys to Storm, his second in command. "Get my bike back to the compound."

He ignored Talon's wicked shout of triumph when Storm tossed them on to him. The younger man's bike was in the shop getting a new paint job. He was the only one there without a ride and the obvious choice to drive Steele's pride and joy home. The smartass better not scratch his chopper. A thought sparked in his brain. "Talon, stay here in the shadows. I need to know if someone comes back for her."

"Like all night? I've got a hot date tonight."

"You *had* a hot date tonight," Steele corrected, fastening a deadly look on him.

Talon took one look at the disheveled woman on the stretcher and agreed. "On it."

"Thanks, Talon. I owe you one."

Stepping up into the ambulance, Steele left everything in the hands of his club. Bonds forged in welded pipes and throbbing motors, Shadowridge Guardians would always have his back just as he would give his life for theirs.

CHAPTER TWO

Blinking her eyes open, Ivy clutched the callused hand in hers. Her gaze searched her surroundings as her heart rate skyrocketed in alarm. Light filtered in through the window, alerting her that the dreadful night had passed. She seemed to be in a hospital.

"Whoa, Little girl. Don't panic. You're okay now," an equally rough voice matched the hand she held as if it were her lifeline.

A name burst from her lips without conscious thought. "Steele!"

"That's me—I'm Steele. Do you remember what your name is?"

"Sir, if you'll move back from the patient, I need to assess her. Her heart rate just alerted me." The firm, no-nonsense voice made them look at the arriving nurse.

"No," Ivy refused, hating the shakiness she heard in her voice.

The nurse stared at her patient lying on the white sheets. "No?"

"I can't let go. He saved me," Ivy explained.

"I see." The nurse looked quickly at the machinery, probably noting that all indicators had settled once again into the safe zones. "I think I can check everything from this side."

Focusing on her patient, her demeanor softened. "I'm Annie. You're at Shadowridge Hospital. Can you tell me what your name is?"

"Ivy? My head's all messed up. I know he's Steele. He saved me," Ivy answered, pressing a hand to her throbbing head. "It hurts. Could I have some medicine?"

"I bet it does. You have an enormous bruise on your temple." The nurse checked her blood pressure and listened to her heart. "Everything sounds good. I'd like to get you up to walk. They cleaned you up the best they could in the emergency department, but I think you'd feel a million times better if you took a shower."

She nodded eagerly and then held her head. The motion made her head hurt worse and her stomach did flip-flops. "Maybe not."

"I'll get you some help and a shower chair. But before everything, let's get you some painkillers that might take the edge off," she suggested.

Ivy would have agreed to anything if it helped with the throbbing, but she wasn't going to nod ever again. "Thank you."

When the nurse bustled out of the room, Ivy turned her head slowly to look at Steele. "You saved me," she repeated.

"You saved yourself. That was smart to make noise so I could find you."

"You're just saying that to make me feel better. It won't work. There was nothing I could do," she admitted with tears instantly coursing down her face as the helplessness she'd felt overwhelmed her.

Without a word, Steele stood to scoop her up in his arms. Mindful of all the wires and tubing attached to her, he settled onto the bed with Ivy on his lap. She could feel the rough fabric of his jeans under her bare bottom where the gown's edges had parted. He rocked her slightly and placed a slightly damp teddy bear into her arms.

"The bear's going to need a better bath, too," he commented, as if her tears didn't bother him at all. "I tried to clean him up with paper towels at the sink."

Wrapped in his brawny arms, Ivy didn't feel at all vulnerable. Who would mess with this man? She laid her aching head on his chest and never wanted to move.

"Can I stay with you for a while? You know, when I get out of here?" When he stopped rocking, she added quickly, "Just for a while. I won't be any trouble."

"Do you think they're coming back?" he questioned.

"They told me I was working for them now."

"How?"

"I work at a bank. They wanted me to help them into the bank after hours. I couldn't do it."

He was silent for what seemed like forever. Finally, he said, "I don't like this, Little girl. They came back to check the dumpster after the bar closed and everyone cleared out. Talon said they searched the dumpster for a while and made a gigantic mess, tossing things out as they looked for you."

"They weren't going to let me get crunched?"

"It appears that they wanted to scare the crap out of you," Steele suggested.

"They did that."

"They endangered you and tortured you. That doesn't happen in Shadowridge. Talon called the cops, but they didn't get there until after the three fled. The cameras in the back of The Hangout might help identify them."

Suddenly, her mind went foggy. She couldn't process anything else. "Steele, I'm having trouble thinking."

"Close your eyes, Ivy. I'll protect you."

"Sir, you're not supposed to be on the bed," the nurse blustered as she returned with two tablets.

"She's scared. I'm here."

The nurse scanned his face and body, taking in the leather cut with the Shadowridge Guardians MC's logo, his tattoos, and take-no-prisoners expression. "You'd be a good person to have on my side if I were in trouble."

"He saved me," Ivy mumbled to the nurse for the third time.

"Here, Ivy. Can you take these for me?" The nurse helped her get them into her mouth and drink some ice water to wash them down.

"I'm glad… Steele was there to help you," Annie commented, reading his name from his cut.

"Save… Not help," Ivy corrected her stubbornly as she closed her eyes to block out the light.

"Got it. Saved," the nurse agreed quietly before returning to her usual brisk tone. "Now, we'll let that medicine take the edge off. With a head injury, the doctor won't give you anything narcotic. I'll get an aide to help you get clean and rustle up a shower chair."

When the room fell quiet again, Ivy whispered, "Is she gone?"

"Just us two chickens here, Little girl."

"You've never been chicken," she answered firmly.

"I don't know. I think I lost a year off my life when I cut open that sack to find you."

"I'm sorry."

"Never be sorry for the evil that others do, Ivy." His tone was firm and brooked no argument.

She patted his thick bicep to both reassure herself and acknowledge the truth of his statement. Ivy could feel his heart beat under her cheek. Time passed as she lay protected in his arms. Ivy was almost asleep when someone new entered the room.

"Ms. Jenkins, I'm Dr. Edwards."

Ivy peeked up at the man in the white coat and knew instantly he'd seen just about everything. The sight of the huge biker holding her in his arms didn't faze him. "Hi."

"I'd like to go over the results of the tests we ran when you came into the emergency department last night. Is it okay to speak freely in front of your companion?"

"Yes. This is Steele. He saved me," Ivy informed him.

"I see. A good man to know," Dr. Edwards acknowledged before referring to the electronic pad in front of him.

"All the tests point to a serious concussion, Ms. Jenkins."

"Call me Ivy," she requested, closing her eyes to block out the light as she attempted to pull her thoughts together to listen closely.

"You're going to have to give her all this in writing, Doc. She's a bit scrambled," Steele recommended.

"Definitely. I'll send her home with thorough directions," the physician agreed before continuing. "All your symptoms should resolve over time, but I can't tell you what that timetable will be. Your brain is going to heal itself, but on its own schedule. Are you safe at home?"

"She's coming to stay with me," Steele answered for Ivy.

"Perfect. I'd like to do an exam to make sure you're okay to go home. If I don't see any extreme reactions, I'll get you out of here today. You'll rest better away from the hospital."

Ivy nodded again and made herself sick. "I've got to stop doing that," she mumbled.

"Does moving your head make you nauseous?" the doctor asked, making a note.

"Badly."

"Unfortunately, that's a normal reaction," he explained before looking at Steele. "Could you set her on the edge of the bed?"

When Steele followed his instructions, Ivy squeezed the bear to her chest and grabbed a handful of his vest before he could move away. Steele shrugged out of his vest and laid it on the bed. "I won't leave without this."

Pulling it onto her lap, Ivy felt the heat from his body covering her bare thighs. With it in place, she followed the doctor's directions to touch his fingers and her nose in a series of tasks. When he asked her to stand, Ivy carefully placed her bear and the cut on the far side of the bed, away from Steele's grasp. Ivy didn't need to worry. He was right at her side, ready to catch her as she wobbled.

"Okay. You can sit back down. If you can have someone with you for the next forty-eight hours, even when you sleep, I'll okay your release from the hospital. No work for a week and then part-time for the week after that. You need to rest and relax. Is that doable?" the doctor asked, carefully watching Ivy and Steele.

"Got it, Doc. She'll be with me."

"I want to see you in two weeks—earlier, if you have any additional symptoms," he warned.

"I'll make sure she gets in to see you," Steele confirmed.

"It will take several hours to get everything organized for your release. Order breakfast and lunch. Rest while you're waiting," the physician recommended. "I know the police have been wanting to talk to you. I'll lift the ban on them interviewing you. Hopefully, they'll find whoever put you in this situation."

When the doctor left to update her chart and sign the release forms, Ivy tugged his vest over her lap to trace the large patch on the back. "You don't have to stay with me," she told him, looking at the frayed material. "I'll be fine."

Reluctantly, she lifted the heavy material to return it to him. "Thanks for saving me."

"I'm sorry you needed saving, Little girl." He shrugged into his cut before surprising her as he lifted her from her perch on the edge of the bed and sat down in the comfy recliner nearby with her in his lap. "Go to sleep. I'm not going anywhere."

Tangling her hand back into the material, she clung to the heavy vest. Exhausted, Ivy rested her head on his broad chest and tumbled into oblivion. Reassured by his closeness, the chatter in her brain quieted.

CHAPTER THREE

"Ready for a shower?" a young woman asked, appearing an hour later with towels and supplies.

"A shower sounds amazing." Ivy pushed herself up from the snuggly position on Steele's chest. Her hand had clamped back onto his vest for reassurance in her sleep.

"You're going to have to let go of me, Little girl, to go get clean."

"You can help her with her shower if you'd like," the nurse's aide chirped helpfully. "We just need to make sure someone is with her in case she gets dizzy. I'd suggest you do the same thing at home for a while as well."

"Will you stay?" Ivy asked and immediately apologized. "I know it's awful of me to ask."

"I'm here. Want me to stand outside the door?"

"Yes," she whispered.

"You got it. Come on." Steele stood and walked her slowly to the bathroom where the nurse's aide took over. He crossed his arms over his chest and stood with his back to the bathroom, blocking anyone from going in.

Her quiet, "Can we leave the door open a bit?" went straight to his heart. Ivy wanted to see him to make sure he was there. To reassure her, he started talking.

"Would you like to know about the people you'll see at the compound?" he asked.

"Yes. Are there a lot? I don't know if I'll remember people's names."

He could tell she was worrying—the exact opposite of what he wanted to achieve. "It's a big compound. We work together and play together. It's like a big dysfunctional family."

"People don't get along?"

"Not always, but we always have each other's back. You'll love Gabriel. While we all pitch in, he's the best cook of the lot. His food will help you heal. He's our chaplain."

"Like a minister?"

Steele chuckled and heard the aide ask Ivy to tilt her head back so she could wet her hair. "He'd be one of the first in line to punish the guys that hurt you. Gabriel takes care of us in a lot of ways."

"I think I'll like him, too. Who's the worst cook?" she asked, obviously intrigued by the men in the club.

"We all do pretty well. You'll love it when Bear's in the kitchen. He loves to spoil the Littles." When she smiled, Steele knew Ivy would look forward to meeting Bear.

"Do you have a position?"

"I'm the president." Steele tried to ignore the splash of water and the knowledge that she was wet and naked. He had a serious talk with his cock, twitching in his jeans, making him almost miss that she'd answered.

"That sounds important."

Not addressing his role in the MC, Steele continued to focus on the people she'd meet. He didn't want her to be scared. "Storm is the vice president. He's the most likely to rampage over anything, but he's also the best friend I've ever had."

"I'm going to like him," Ivy said confidently. "Who's the scariest?"

"Kade," Steele answered without hesitation. "He's our enforcer. You can bet he already has people out looking for the guys that did this."

The door bumped against him. "Sir, I need to get some ointment and bandages to treat the scratches. She'll be fine enjoying the heat of the shower for a second with you there."

Immediately, Steele moved away. He didn't count on the aide opening the door quite as much and caught a glimpse of Ivy sitting naked with her head tilted back into the water, allowing it to course over her. *Fuck!* His shaft twitched against his fly at that thought, and he reined in his control once again.

"I know I'll like Kade. I'd love for those guys to be found. Who don't you like?" she asked perceptively.

"Not a question of like, but more of trust. Virtually everyone I trust one hundred percent. There's one guy…" Steele shut up. She didn't know all the group politics. The other members didn't have a problem with the one he didn't trust. Maybe it was just him.

This time, he shifted so he wouldn't see her when the aide returned to finish her shower. Steele heard the water turn off and the sound of material being unfolded before being wrapped around her. Ivy thanked the aide for helping her get clean.

"I'm glad to help. Let me put some medicine on those scratches. And we'll get you back in bed to rest until all the paperwork is complete."

"Is there anything I could wear home?" Ivy asked, and Steele cursed himself for not thinking of this.

"There's a bag at the nurses' desk for you that someone just dropped off."

"Really? Do you know who?" Ivy asked.

"Someone named Carlee. I usually don't remember names, but that's so pretty. It's spelled with two E's at the end," the chatty aide supplied.

"I don't know a Carlee," Ivy said weakly.

Steele could tell her energy was gone. "All dressed?" he

asked, turning around to look in the door just as the aide fastened the tie around her neck loosely. He strode in to pick up Ivy as she struggled to continue standing and carried her toward the bed.

"Let me change those sheets before she lies down. She'll just get dirty again."

Steele changed course and cradled her on his lap in the recliner. Resting her head on his shoulder, he felt her relax against him. In a few minutes, the aide changed the bed and collected the bag from the nurses' desk. Carlee had brought Ivy some clothes to wear. He pulled out his phone to update everyone and send Carlee his thanks.

"I'm not going to like him either," Ivy mumbled when the room was quiet. It took Steele a minute to realize that she was talking about the guy they'd discussed last. "Don't tell me his name. I'll try to figure it out."

"It's best if you rest in my room or stay with me when I'm working."

"With you," she mumbled without hesitation as she drifted into another catnap.

Holding her gently against his frame, Steele knew there were a million other things he could do, but only this one was important. This wisp of a girl whose damp hair soaked his T-shirt occupied the top of the list. He could depend on his second-in-command, Storm, to take care of anything vital for a few hours.

His phone buzzed, and Steele moved carefully to grab it and look at the screen. Storm. The manager at The Hangout had allowed him to view the security tape. A van had pulled close to the dumpster, and the sack had been tossed inside. The van was gone in a flash. The license plate showed in the tape, but something covered the letters and numbers, making it unreadable.

There are hundreds of white vans in the city, Steele thought to himself. They'd have to find them another way. Quickly, he texted his instructions:

> Check to see if there are any security cameras on the buildings on the path from the bank to the bar. One focused on the bank parking lot would be the most beneficial.

A thumbs up symbol appeared and Steele knew Storm would look into all possibilities.

CHAPTER FOUR

"Officer, I'm sorry I can't give you a better description. If I heard their voices again, I know I'd recognize them," Ivy commented.

She'd moved to sit on the edge of her bed when they'd walked in. Steele had quickly corralled the billowing fabric of her hospital gown to keep her from flashing the officers. Curiously, Ivy hadn't been embarrassed to have Steele take care of her. She'd felt better when the large man had stood by her side.

"If you remember anything, even something that doesn't seem important, call us," the detective requested, handing Ivy his card.

"I will. Promise!"

"We're concerned about your safety as these guys are still out there," the other police officer warned.

"She'll stay with me," Steele said in a tone that brooked no arguments.

"At the Guardians' compound?" the first questioned.

"Yes."

"You can't get any safer than that," the second detective assured. "We did stop at the bank and got the video footage."

"The bank! I haven't even called them," Ivy said, raising a hand to whack herself on the forehead for being a dunce.

"None of that, Little girl," Steele corrected, grabbing her hand before it could reach its target.

"Looks like you're in excellent hands," the second officer noted. "We'll be in touch. We have your purse and phone from the back entrance of the bank. They'll be held for evidence for a while."

"Thank you, detectives," Ivy said quickly as they left. It was a funny feeling to be glad she had Steele in her corner. She had the impression the officers' hands would be tied in how much they could do.

Peeking up at Steele, she guessed he would operate outside the law. "Why do you want to help me?"

"It's what we do, Little girl. The Guardians are here to protect the vulnerable in Shadowridge."

She bristled at that statement. "I'm not vulnerable."

"Someone has decided you are. Just think of me as your backup. Everyone needs someone to have their back."

"Is that what the other members do? Are they going to be okay with me staying with you? I don't want to invade a men-only cave."

"There are other women there, Ivy—old ladies and daughters are welcome in the compound."

"Like grandmas?" she asked in fascination.

"Old ladies have nothing to do with age. It's a wife or a long-term girlfriend of a member of the MC."

"Oh!"

"Um, Steele?" she added.

"Hmm?" Steele asked, rubbing the muscles in the back of her neck with one hand.

"Do you have an old lady?"

"I don't. I've been looking for someone special. My own Little girl."

"You have a daughter?" she asked, puzzled.

Steele shook his head before grinning at her. "A Little girl with a capital L for Little. That's different than a daughter."

Suddenly, her scrambled brains clicked into place. "Like a submissive?" she whispered.

"Yes. A special kind of one."

"You're a Daddy?" she asked, mentally capitalizing the D.

"Ivy! We've been so worried about you," a smooth polished voice announced loudly from the doorway, making her grimace as it echoed inside her skull.

"Talk quietly," Steele ordered.

The suited gentleman in the doorway looked taken aback for a second before he continued to talk to Ivy in a slightly softer tone. "When the police showed up at the bank this morning to obtain the video footage, we understood why you neglected your duties and didn't show up this morning."

The rebuke in his voice was tangible, making Ivy respond immediately, "My apologies, Mr. Harris. I should have called."

"Mr. Harris, is it? You understand that Ivy was abducted, abused, and her life was in jeopardy because of the lack of security at your bank?" Steele said, the judgement in his tone ringing clearly.

"Well, definitely, Ivy should have followed the security protocols. Nevertheless, I was concerned to hear that you had been injured," the man answered, sloughing off any responsibility.

"I did nothing wrong, Mr. Harris. I checked the viewfinder before leaving. I didn't share the new security codes and ended up tied, bagged, and thrown into a dumpster to be crushed," Ivy said defensively. Her headache flared back into excruciating territory as her blood pressure rose. She closed her eyes and pressed a hand against her forehead as she swayed.

"You need to leave," Steele said in a tone that made the bank president take a step back. "Ivy's doctors have banned her from working for at least a week to allow her brain to recover."

"Be sure to get that in writing, Ivy. We'll need documentation of the doctor's orders to allow you to use your sick time."

"Leave now. You won't dock her sick leave. You won't threaten her job status. You will be very supportive," Steele stated firmly as he walked forward to force the unsympathetic man to back up to the door.

"I don't know who you are, sir—" Mr. Harris began when Steele interrupted him.

"I can be your worst nightmare if you don't handle this correctly," Steele said ominously before closing the door in the man's face.

He returned to Ivy's side and lifted her legs up to the bed as he helped her stretch out. When the covers were tucked around her chin, Steele rang the nurse and requested pain medication. Pulling the chair up to the bed, he sat next to her.

Needing comfort as her brain pounded inside her skull, Ivy snuck a hand from under the covers to grab his cut. She clamped her fingers around the material and held on tight. Gratefully taking the tablets when they were held to her mouth, she tumbled into sleep.

"They're still going to let me go home?" she asked, a couple of hours later when the nurse returned with her discharge papers.

"Yes. At home, you'll be protected from annoying visitors," the nurse predicted. "I have a list of your discharge instructions to review with you. There's just one change from what the doctor said earlier. After hearing the result from your boss visiting, he's extended your time away from the bank for a full two weeks and warns he may add more time. You need to stay as peaceful as possible to allow your brain to heal."

"I'm so fired," Ivy whispered.

"He also sent a copy of his instructions to his golf partner, who sits on the board at the bank," Annie informed them with a smirk.

"Mr. Harris won't like that," Ivy said, trying not to feel triumphant that the doctor had gone over his head.

"It doesn't matter. He's done his best to make sure your job is safe for as long as you need to heal," Annie assured her. "Let me go over these instructions with you, and then we'll get you ready to go home."

In a few minutes, the paperwork was complete. Annie removed all the monitors on her skin and the IV. The relief in getting the needle out of her arm made her head feel better, and Ivy giggled at the ridiculousness of that connection. Glancing up, she found Steele watching her with a smile.

Damn. He was attractive, all scowly and protective. But that grin made her heart do flip-flops. She ducked her head down so she wouldn't give her thoughts away.

"That will make getting dressed easier! I'll have someone come escort you to the entrance in a few minutes," Annie said before bustling away.

Holding out the hem of the hospital gown, Ivy commented, "I don't know what happened to my clothes."

"They cut them off in the emergency department. They were ruined anyway," Steele told her, remembering the alcohol and muck-soaked garments he'd found her in.

"I don't remember a lot about that night," Ivy admitted. "Just being terrified and their voices."

"Maybe that's best. Are you ready to get dressed and go check out the Guardians' complex?"

"Yes. They've been really nice here, but…"

"It's a hospital. You'll sleep better when you're out of here," he said when her voice trailed away.

She watched him open the sack the nurse had brought in and pull out several items. The gray sweatpants looked so comfortable and warm. They made her instantly wish to get rid of the thin hospital gown. The thoughtful donor had included a T-shirt emblazoned with the same logo on Steele's cut. Ivy traced the tough cartoon bear with her fingertip.

"Is it okay if I wear this?" she asked.

"If it's been given to you, of course. You have a tie with us now," Steele answered, studying her face as he spoke.

Ivy felt a tear roll down her cheek, and she dashed it away. "Thank you for everything." They'd all been so wonderful.

"No tears. When Carlee heard what had happened, she thought of bringing clothes. She wanted to help. You all are about the same size, so it works well. Let's get you dressed."

"Are you going to help me?" Ivy asked, feeling overwhelmed by the simple task, but embarrassed to have him see her naked.

"I am. I'll close my eyes," he promised.

"Oh, that will be okay, then."

She picked up the panties and noted the tags were still on the garment. "Can you take these off? Better do that with your eyes open," she teased and then gasped as he pulled a large knife from his boot to slice through the thin plastic strips holding onto the tags.

"What do you use that for?" popped out of her mouth before she could stop it.

"There are some things Little girls don't need to know." That answer didn't reassure her, but he distracted her by kneeling at her feet to hold out the panties for her to step into.

"Sorry, my legs are stubbly," she whispered as he drew them up her calves.

"Stand up, Ivy," he requested, dismissing her apology as unimportant with a shake of his head and boosting her to her feet.

Bracing herself on his shoulders, Ivy watched him close his eyes deliberately as he drew the panties up under her gown. His fingers smoothed the soft cotton fabric into position over her hips and waist before grabbing the sweatpants and helping her step into them.

Wrapped in the cuddly fabric, Ivy felt more like herself.

Less vulnerable. She turned to grab the stretchy sports bra the kind woman had included and followed Steele's guidance to turn and face the bed for him to untie the strings of her hospital gown. When he let the institutional garment sag away from her body, Ivy pulled the bra over her head and struggled to get it into place, losing her balance. Steele wrapped an arm around her waist, steadying her as he gathered her hair from where it dangled behind her and helped her move the back strap into position. Quickly, Ivy shifted her small breasts into place.

"Sit back on the bed, Ivy. Don't exhaust yourself," Steele directed, helping her move to that position before draping the T-shirt over her head.

"I don't suppose they saved my shoes?" she asked.

"You weren't wearing shoes," he answered.

"I wasn't? Maybe the police have those with my things. Think I'll get them back? I don't know if I can live without my phone."

"No electronics for at least a week, Little girl. I'll get you an emergency phone to use if you need it until you get yours back."

"I'll pay you back for everything," Ivy rushed to tell him, feeling guilty.

"Not happening."

She couldn't argue because her aide entered with a wheelchair to escort her to the front entrance of the hospital.

Steele's hand smoothed over the back of her head. "The guys dropped off my truck. I'll go get it and meet you at the entrance."

Ivy nodded.

"You won't leave her alone?" Steele half asked, half demanded of the aide.

"I'm required to stay with Ivy until you pick her up," she promised.

Steele raised Ivy's chin with his callused hand until their gazes met again. "I'll get there soon. Stay with the aide."

When he left, Ivy quickly asked the kind woman who had helped her with the shower, "Can I go to the bathroom?"

"Of course."

When she got back into the wheelchair, Ivy looked around the hospital room as the aide set a few supplies, the teddy bear, and the folder with her orders on Ivy's lap to take home. It seemed like her whole life had changed here. Ivy wondered if she'd ever get her self-confidence back. Now she was just scared. What else could be waiting to harm her out there?

CHAPTER
FIVE

Snagging the teddy bear in one hand, Steele lifted the sleeping woman from the truck and carried her into the back entrance of the clubhouse. It was late enough that most of the Guardians would have left the shop by this time. He didn't want to overwhelm her with a ton of people to meet.

Heading for his apartment, Steele avoided running into anyone. The level of conversation and noise coming from the gathering areas didn't disturb her sleep. He juggled her slight body to open and close the door, isolating them inside. Once at the bedside, he tossed the covers aside and set Ivy on the sheets. Immediately, she rolled onto her tummy and buried her face in the soft pillow. Steele placed the teddy bear next to her.

"Steele," she mumbled, pulling the stuffed friend close.

"I'm here, Little girl. Go back to sleep."

"I wish he was my Daddy," Ivy confided before dropping back into a deep sleep, leaving Steele rocked back on his heels.

He'd hardened his heart over the years, dismissing his possibility of finding a Little girl of his own. Could this horrible attack on the adorable woman have allowed them to find each other?

Forcing himself to move, he lifted a chair from the corner of the room and carried it to the bed. Steel lowered himself into the upholstered seat and watched Ivy sleep. After several minutes, he heard a knock on the outer door to the apartment. When he answered, Storm greeted him.

"The sensors told us you were home. How is she?" Storm asked as he handed Steele a delicious-smelling, laden tray.

"Sleeping. She has a severe concussion from banging her head against the dumpster. It's rattled everything inside her. She'll stay with us for a while," Steele shared.

"Good. We'll monitor for anyone hanging around. Did you see anything on your way home?"

"Nothing. But there was a lot of traffic. It would be easy to hide," Steele noted.

"They'd be stupid to come here."

"They were stupid to take her. Mistreating her doomed them," Steele pointed out.

The men exchanged a look, promising retribution for the kidnappers' actions. Steele added, "She's mine, Storm."

"Yours?"

"My Little girl."

"Damn. I'm glad you found her, but…" Storm put a hand on Steele's shoulder and squeezed before changing the subject. "We'll try to keep the noise down so she can sleep."

"Thanks. I think she's out for the night. No one sleeps well in the hospital."

"Eat. You'll need your strength."

Closing the door behind Storm, Steele placed the tray on the counter and explored the contents. Bear had smoked a brisket. After living on the food he'd ordered brought with Ivy's meals in the hospital, the slices of tender meat demanded his attention. Steele quickly wolfed down a large portion of it and all the extras before placing the rest in the fridge for Ivy when she woke up.

He returned to the bedroom and tucked the covers under Ivy's chin before sitting in the chair. Steele divided his attention between Ivy and catching up with the messages and emails that had clogged his mailbox. Storm had handled everything urgent. He owed his second-in-command.

When darkness settled, Steele took a quick shower and climbed into bed next to Ivy. Almost immediately, she gravitated to his warmth and cuddled against his chest. Tamping down his body's response, Steele wrapped an arm around her and closed his eyes.

She needs rest.

He dozed between her movements. Totally attuned to her breathing and motions, Steele woke each time she wiggled. Each time, she got a bit closer to him until she plastered herself against his skin.

"No! NO!" Her frightened shout jerked him to attention.

"Ivy, you're safe."

"Don't! I don't want to be in that sack! No! Let me out! Where are you taking me? Let me go!"

"Wake up, Little girl," he urged, rubbing his hands over her back to drag her from the nightmare assault replaying in her mind.

"Where am I? Did you throw me in the trash?" she whimpered.

"Ivy, open your eyes!" he ordered, thundering into the quiet of the darkness.

"What?" she mumbled. "Where am I?"

"You're safe, Little girl. You're here with me at the Shadowridge Guardians' compound," Steele replied, intentionally giving her information to focus on.

"Steele?"

"That's right, Emerald Eyes. You're safe now."

"Why did they do that to me?" she wailed.

"Because they're bad people. They won't bother you again."

"You can't know that for sure. I can't hide here with you forever," she said miserably.

"Why not?"

Even in the darkness, he watched her search his face to see if he was telling the truth. He stroked a hand over her rumpled hair. "We need to talk, Little girl, but I think you're mine. I don't let go of things that are mine."

"You think you're my Daddy?" she whispered.

He knew it was easier for her to hide in the darkness and ask. "I know I'm your Daddy. Let me take care of you."

Feeling her nod slowly, Steele stroked over her spine to reassure her. "Are you hungry?"

"No. I'm so tired."

"Go back to sleep, Ivy. I'll watch over you."

Rubbing her back in slow sweeps of his hand, Steele felt the tension ease from her body as she relaxed against him.

"Daddy," she mumbled against his chest, making his heart skip a beat as he watched over her.

Steele pressed a light kiss to her hair and squeezed her a bit tighter as a reward. He didn't know how this had happened, but he wouldn't question it. Ever.

A stuffie bonked into his face, jolting Steele from his sleep. Dismissing the threat, Steele checked on the precious woman lying draped over his chest. She still snoozed deeply. He eased himself from under her as she grumbled at his movement. Retaking his seat on the chair, he made plans.

An hour later, he watched her hand search for him. "I'm here, Ivy." To his delight, she crawled from under the covers to clamber onto his lap and wrap her arms around his neck.

"I dreamed I was alone."

"I'm here." Steele brushed the hair from her face. "How do you feel?"

"My head hurts," she confessed. "I should take some medicine."

"Let's go get it."

Standing with her in his arms, Steele carried her into the bathroom and stood her next to the vanity. He opened the medicine cabinet to reveal the over-the-counter tablets the doctor had prescribed for the pain. When he turned on the water, she squirmed.

"Go potty, Little girl."

Instantly, she fled to the toilet and returned a few minutes later with a red face. Steele didn't comment but turned on the water for her to wash her hands. When she had finished, he handed her the tablets and watched her take them.

"Breakfast?" he asked and heard her stomach growl in response. "I'll take that as a yes. Let's brush your hair and wash your face."

"I can do it."

"Let Daddy."

"I didn't dream that?" she asked.

"No, Little girl." Steele picked up a brush from the counter and stroked it through her deep brown hair. When the silky strands hung smoothly down her back, he quickly washed her face, taking extreme care not to touch the livid bruising on the side of her head. He wanted to kill whoever had hurt her.

"It's okay, Steele. I'll heal," she whispered.

"They're not getting away with this, Little girl," he vowed.

Quickly, he got himself ready as well. Taking her hand, he led her to the door. When she hesitated, he asked, "What's wrong, sweetheart?"

"Are there other people out there?"

"I'm sure there are a few. Everyone gathers for breakfast."

"Other women?"

"Maybe a few. Why?"

She scanned his appearance. He wore a loose pair of thin cotton sleep pants. "Could you put on a shirt?" Ivy whispered.

"You don't want me out there without a shirt?"

"Please?"

Steele returned to the bedroom and grabbed a shirt. Walking back to her side as he pulled it on, Steele watched her staring at his bare chest until he buttoned it completely. He stifled a laugh and didn't allow a smile to curve his lips. Modesty wasn't a big thing around the compound.

"Let's go."

CHAPTER SIX

After a run to her house to get clothes, shoes, and supplies, Ivy looked up at the motorcycle repair shop sign as Steele parked his truck in front of it. Instantly, she felt relieved to be back where she was safe.

Ivy had worried about getting into her home but thank goodness she had an electronic lock on the front door and had automatically remembered the pattern to punch in the code. Her house keys should still be in her purse with her phone. Ivy crossed her fingers, hoping the police would return them soon.

As they exited the car next to the clubhouse, a mechanic from the shop yelled, "Steele! I need that set of pipes. Can you get that done soon?"

"I'll get on it tomorrow," Steele promised.

"I could really use it today."

Terrified by the thought of being separated from him, Ivy rushed to say, "I could go with you."

"Doc can work on another project, Ivy. They don't need me today," Steele assured her before sending a meaningful look at the man who'd approached.

She saw him open his mouth and snap it shut when Steele shook his head slightly. "Is there somewhere I can hang out while you work? I don't mind sitting against the wall. I'll stay out of the way," she promised.

"There are plenty of chairs, Little girl."

"Then let's go there and you can get something done," she suggested, feeling like she was a total bother. The last thing she wanted to do was disrupt his life any more than she had already.

Reluctantly, Steele took her to the shop where work had piled up for him during his temporary absence. He worried about the noise, but she agreed to wear a pair of headphones to muffle the sound. Seated in the best office chair in the work area, Ivy pretended to admire the motorcycles pictured inside the magazine as she flipped through the pages.

The play of muscles under the protective gear Steele wore fascinated her. He'd shown her all the equipment he used while welding as he prepared to work. Ivy watched him flip the protective helmet into place as he arced the torch to create a molten bead of metal that joined the pieces together as if they were one. The glowing metal scared her, but Steele worked confidently and efficiently. Her fingers remembered the feel of scars on his skin. Had that deadly torch caused those?

As if he felt her eyes on him, Steele looked up when he finished a seam. Extinguishing the flame, he flipped the visor up and asked, "You okay, Little girl?"

Lifting one earpiece away from her ear, she answered, "I'm good."

"Ready to nap?" he asked.

"I couldn't lie there, could I?" she asked, pointing at the crash bed the Guardians had stashed in the corner for whoever needed it.

"Let me get a fresh blanket." Steele nodded at Storm working nearby and received an acknowledgement. Ivy knew immediately Steele had asked him to keep an eye on her.

When he returned with a big fluffy comforter and a pillow, she curled up on the bed and dropped immediately into sleep. She only woke when Steele picked her up.

"I can walk," she protested before, "Ew! You smell," popped out of her mouth. Ivy clapped a hand over her lips in embarrassment.

Steele laughed as he set Ivy on her feet and took her hand, leading her into the Guardians' living space. "Sorry, Little girl. Let me go take a shower before dinner."

"I'm sorry. I shouldn't have said that."

"It's the truth. You should always tell your Daddy the truth."

"Amen!" a large gruff man commented from the side of the room, looking deliberately at a pretty Goth girl who Ivy had met at the large breakfast gathering.

"Dad! He's talking about her *Daddy*, not a dad," Remi said in exasperation, causing the older man to chuckle.

Ivy rushed to follow Steele. As soon as they were alone in the hallway, she hissed, "They all know?"

When Steele nodded, she asked, "About us or about Daddies in general?"

"Both."

Shell-shocked, Ivy followed Steele into the apartment. As she tried to process that information through her jumbled brain, she stepped out of her sneakers while he toed off his heavy boots, leaving them next to the door. Trailing him through the rooms, Ivy watched Steele turn on the water to warm.

The sight of him stripping off his shirt totally distracted her. When his fingers unbuttoned his jeans, she whirled around, making herself dizzy. She should not be watching him undress.

"Whoa!" She steadied herself against the door frame.

"Shower time, Little girl."

His hands lifted the borrowed T-shirt she'd slept in and still wore. Automatically, she lifted her arms to let him tug it off. "Are we going to shower together?" she squeaked as he turned her gently around to face him.

"You are too dizzy to shower by yourself," he answered simply before pushing her sweatpants over her hips.

When his fingers hooked into the sides of her panties, she

slapped her hands over his. "I'm not really anything to look at," she said self-consciously, not wishing to disappoint him.

Steele turned his hand to capture hers. Pulling it gently forward, he placed her hand against his pelvis. His hard shaft jutted through the opening in the material under her hand. Without thinking, her fingers moved automatically to attempt to wrap around his erection. She squeezed, feeling the thickness of the rigid shaft.

"Little girl," he growled, and she let go of him as if his flesh were on fire.

Quickly, Steele removed the last of her clothing and helped her step free. He slid the jeans down his muscular thighs and kicked them away. After dealing with his socks and tossing the pile of their clothing into the hamper, Steele urged her into the walk-in shower.

It was huge with two showerheads. Groaning in delight, Ivy stepped under one and stuck her face into the cascade of water. She felt Steele's skin brush against hers and she looked over her shoulder to see him so close.

The expanse of his body mesmerized her. Ivy scanned his physique, honed by work and an obvious workout routine. She'd seen the large fitness room where the Guardians worked out. *Steele must live in there.*

"Oh, what big eyes you have, Little girl."

"Sorry!" Ivy slammed her eyes shut and wobbled unbalanced in the shower stall. Reaching out for something to steady her, she grabbed his thick biceps.

"Let me see those beautiful green eyes, Ivy," he gently reprimanded her.

"I keep staring at you."

"I'm a big boy. I can handle a bit of staring."

"Big?" She seized on that word and giggled.

Opening her eyes, she peeked at his face and tried to keep her gaze focused there.

His lips twisted into an amused smirk. "Let's get you clean."

Grabbing an old-fashioned bar of white soap, Steele rubbed it over her skin with one hand and spread the lather with the other. When she tilted off balance, he steadied her against his hard frame. Ivy could feel his cock pressing into her side.

"Eep!" she squeaked as he whisked the bar between her buttocks before his hand followed to clean her. Steele wrapped his arm holding the soap around her waist to hold her steady.

"Nothing is off limits to your Daddy."

Ivy nodded without thinking. She started to protest, but realized that this had always been her fantasy. To have someone who cared so much about her that he took care of her completely. His fingers brushed over that small entrance hidden between her buttocks, and Ivy gritted her teeth to avoid moaning.

His fingertip poked slightly inside, making the ring of muscles burn from the touch of the soap. She rose onto her toes, freezing at the feel of his beard as he leaned forward to remind her, "Daddy is in charge." Before she could agree or disagree, he guided her to turn around, and the water pelted over her sensitized skin.

She watched with anticipation as Steele rotated the soap in his powerful hands. Ivy could almost feel his gaze brush over her skin as he scanned her body while building up a lather. Locking her gaze on his face, she watched his expression as he washed the front of her body. The desire burning in his eyes blazed hotter as he touched her. His hands glided over her collarbones and shoulders before sliding down her arms. Spreading her fingers, he massaged her hands, making her whole body relax.

Gripping her waist lightly, Steele pulled her closer. She watched, holding her breath as he lowered his lips to capture hers. Ivy opened her mouth, inviting him to deepen the sweet kiss he gave her. Immediately, Steele swept his tongue over her inner lips to taste her before sliding inside. Ivy loved his flavor and rose onto her tiptoes to wrap her arms around his neck.

She moaned when his tongue tangled with hers seductively.

His kiss was perfect—not too aggressive, not too saliva-drenched, not too timid. The scratch of his surprisingly soft beard added more sensations to the exchange. Steele knew how to kiss, and he did it well.

When he lifted his head, Ivy protested, clutching his shoulders to stay close. "Daddy?" She was shocked how easily that title came to her lips.

"We'll play more, Little girl. Let's get both of us clean."

Steele stroked the soap over her torso before handing it to her. "You help Daddy, Little girl. Would you like to wash my chest?" he asked.

Jumping at the offer to touch him, Ivy rubbed the bar over his chest hair and along that trailing line down his chiseled abdomen before handing it back to him. She smoothed the slick lather over his skin, enjoying the feel of his muscles under her fingertips. When her hands drifted toward his pelvis, Steele's hand trapped hers gently against his hard stomach.

"That's not my chest," he pointed out.

"I know, but…" She let her voice trail away suggestively.

"Ask for permission, Little girl," he answered, lifting his hand from hers.

"Permission?" she echoed.

He nodded in answer as his hands spread suds over her small, sensitive breasts. Distracted by his touch, Ivy hesitated for a few seconds before pulling her thoughts back together. "I need to ask permission to touch your…?" Somehow saying it sounded so dirty.

"Cock? Yes."

Ivy stared at him. Steele wasn't perturbed at all by using that word. So, she could use it too.

"Daddy, can I touch your cock?" she asked saucily, making a joke of it.

"Not with that tone, you can't." His face was solemn. He wasn't joking.

"I can't?"

"Nope." Steele rubbed the bar over the mound at the V of her legs and spread it over her lower lips. "Spread your legs."

Automatically, she shifted her legs apart and closed her eyes at the sensations he aroused in her as he spread the cleanser through her pink folds. The difference in the rules between him touching her and Ivy not being allowed to touch him made her try to resist the sensations he caused. "That's not fair."

"Daddies make the rules. Try again but ask nicely," he suggested.

"Daddy, can I touch your cock?" she sassed.

"Nope." His fingers stroking her made her eyes cross.

"Daddy, can I touch your cock?" she asked in mock anger. Who could be angry with a man who had a magic touch?

"No."

Lifting onto her tiptoes as the sensations built between her legs, Ivy gasped in need. "Daddy, can I touch your cock?"

"Yes, Little girl."

Her hand closed around his thickness. He groaned as she squeezed him experimentally. Stroking her hand toward the tip, Ivy struggled to divide her attention between giving and receiving pleasure. Her brain rebelled, and she froze. As if he could read her distress, Steele shifted her hand away, turned her around before pulling her back tightly against his chest.

His fingers returned to their skilled play between her legs as he supported her body. Focusing completely on the sensations of the warm shower spray striking her skin, the feel of his hard body pressed against her, and the tingling that built between her legs, Ivy dropped her head back against his chest and closed her eyes. In a flash, those growing zings of pleasure exploded inside her and she shuddered in his arms. His touch gentled as he prolonged her enjoyment.

When his lips pressed against her temple, Ivy pulled herself together. She could feel his thick erection pressing into her bottom and felt remorse that she hadn't showered him with as much pleasure as Steele had lavished on her.

"I'm sorry," she whispered.

"For being injured? Never apologize for that, Little girl."

His callused hands whisked over her body, removing all the suds from her skin before wrapping her in a towel. "Lean against the wall. I'll be quick."

Given permission to remain in the shower with him, Ivy followed his directions and lounged in the dry area of the shower. Watching his powerful hands finish cleaning his body, she tried to memorize his unbelievable physique. How could anyone who looked like that naked want someone like her?

"Stop it."

She lifted her gaze to his face. "What?"

"Stop judging yourself as lacking."

Staring at him in disbelief, Ivy watched him tilt his head back into the spray, as if he hadn't just read her mind. He couldn't really know what she was thinking, could he?

When he emerged from the spray, Steele stalked forward to grab the other towel and scrub his body and hair dry. Turning to her, he tilted her chin up with one hand before pressing an intense kiss to her lips. Instantly, desire rekindled inside her.

"You are everything I desire. I won't allow anyone to be mean to you—not even you, Little girl. Understand?"

"Y-Yes!" She stumbled over the word as he unwrapped her like the most precious present a man could ever receive. She closed her eyes to focus on the sensations as he rubbed the soft fabric over her skin.

"Bedtime, Little girl."

Her eyelids opened, and she stared at him. "I don't want to go to bed. I just woke up from a nap," she protested.

"I didn't say you were going to sleep."

Steele scooped her up gently in his arms and carried Ivy to the large bed. Sweeping the covers away, he placed her resting on her back with her bottom at the edge of the mattress. She propped up her torso on her elbows as he made a space for himself, kneeling on the floor between her legs.

"Isn't it time for dinner?" she asked nervously.

"Yes."

Steele lowered his lips to press a kiss on her mound. Instinctively, she tried to pull her legs together, but he controlled them firmly how he wanted them. She held her breath, waiting to see what he intended to do.

"My Little girl needs pleasure. It's too much for your brain to give and receive at the same time."

He traced the cleft of her pussy with the tip of his tongue. "Mmm," he hummed. "Delicious."

Spreading her thighs wider, he pressed his mouth against her and explored. Searching for those touches and spots that brought her the most pleasure, Steele rebuilt the desire and passion that had filled her in the shower. Overwhelmed, she lowered herself off her elbows to lie flat on the mattress.

"Close your eyes," he directed before returning to tantalizing Ivy.

Focused completely on the pleasure he offered her, small cries of need escaped from her throat as she grabbed a handful of the sheet below her to ground herself. A thick finger pressed into her, making Ivy arch her hips upward toward the invader. Instantly, he restricted her movement, clamping a hand over one of her thighs to pin her to the mattress.

She loved the feel of being restrained. It freed her from having to think about what she should do—how she should react. Ivy could do nothing but feel as he focused on her clit, lashing it with the tip of his tongue until all those sizzles of pleasure coalesced. Her orgasm hovered just out of her reach.

Protesting with soft sounds, she tried to move slightly to find what she needed to push her into the climax that eluded her. That finger stroking inside her became two, stretching her body to allow both to enter. The rough calluses on his fingers rubbed over the most sensitive spots inside her. When his lips sealed around her clit and sucked, she exploded into a million pieces.

Her torso jerked up from the surface of the bed. Steele moved quickly to wrap a hand around her skull, cushioning her head from crashing back down to the mattress. Stretched over her, he pinned her under his body weight. He didn't distract her from the pleasure—just insured that she would be safe from injuring herself more.

When her body calmed, he stood to lift her into his arms before settling back against the headboard. Sitting on his lap, Ivy absorbed all the kisses and hugs as she lay against his chest. When his phone buzzed, she pulled herself from the afterglow.

"Sorry, Little girl," he apologized as he glanced at the name that appeared on his watch. He accepted the call, and she listened carefully to his side of the conversation, trying to fill in the gaps.

"Storm? What's up?"

"No, no need to bring us food. We'll be down in five to join everyone."

CHAPTER SEVEN

"You could go on without me," she suggested as he gently pulled a T-shirt over her head. Ivy tried to focus on something other than the scenic view of Steele in low-slung jeans and nothing else.

"Not going to happen, Little girl. You need food to heal."

"There's a lot of people out there I don't know. And, I look like this," she protested, waving a hand over her body.

"You don't need a suit and heels here, Little girl. That would look out of place. Don't worry about who's out there. You met most of them at the shop today," he said and treated the scratches from the rope bindings around her ankles one last time before fitting slippers over her feet. She glanced at her wrists which had healed quickly.

She watched him grab a T-shirt from a drawer and tug it on. "Aren't you going to wear underwear?" Ivy whispered as he held a hand out to help her stand.

"No one will know but you. It will be our secret," he said, obviously trying to stop himself from grinning.

"I liked your friends. They were nice to me today."

"Good. They'll be nice to you tonight, too."

He guided her out into the hallway and toward the voices

she could already hear. She paused, and he stopped immediately. "What's wrong?"

"Don't you want to lock your door?"

"Locks aren't necessary here, Little girl. No one would think of taking another member's stuff. If they needed something, they would ask."

"How about someone else coming in?"

"Come with me, Ivy." He led her to the doorway and stopped to allow her to look at the crowd assembled inside the large room. "Who's going to get past those guys?"

She looked at the massively muscled men filling the kitchen and already seated around the table. Who would consider messing with these guys and, even if they did, who would survive? "I see what you mean."

"You're safe here, Ivy. Let's stop and get something special for you. Then you'll feel like this is your home, too," Steele suggested.

"Like what?"

"Come look." He drew her to a closed door. Opening it, he revealed shelves and racks filled with unique items. Blankets, cups, bowls, bibs, and a lot of things she didn't recognize. She tried to pretend she didn't see the padded items on the bottom shelf.

"This is Little girl stuff," she said in amazement.

"It is. This is where your blanket came from for the shop. Tonight, let's pick out a cup for you. Choose your favorite design and no one will use it but you."

Ivy scanned the shelves and noticed a cup with a pretty girl with dark hair and vivid green eyes. "She looks like me!"

"Great choice." Steele scooped it up and picked up a matching top. He also collected an item wrapped in a plastic wrapper and stashed it in his pocket.

"What was that?" she asked.

"Something for later. Come get something to eat." Drawing her into the main area, Steele put his hands over Ivy's ears to shield her before announcing, "Everyone, meet Ivy. She's mine."

A roar of welcomes and smiles flowed over her as the club members responded to Steele's announcement. She even heard some congratulations and comments that it was about time. Ivy peeked up at the fierce-looking man next to her. Steele didn't mean to keep her, did he?

Ivy slipped her hand into his when he dropped his protective hands back to his sides. She relaxed when he squeezed her fingers lightly. The group was mainly men, but there were several women gathered there as well. Two very different-looking young women stood and walked over to greet Ivy personally. One she recognized as Remi. Ivy had met her that morning at breakfast and also run into her again with her dad.

"Hi, I'm Carlee," said the other woman. She was adorable and wore her hair in pigtails.

"Nice to see you again," said the Goth-looking girl named Remi.

"Thank you for the clothes, Carlee. I'll get them washed and back to you," Ivy promised.

"No rush. I was glad to help. Come on. Let us introduce you to the women."

Feeling like she should follow, Ivy trailed behind the two women, leaving Steele's protective presence and shielding hands.

"Some are daughters like me. That's my dad, Rock," Remi shared, pointing to the large older man who looked exactly like his name. Even his skin seemed a touch gray.

"Is your dad a member, too, Carlee?" Ivy asked, trying to make conversation.

"No. Remi and I have been best friends since kindergarten. I grew up hanging around here. I guess I'm adopted?" Carlee answered easily, with a smile and a shrug.

"Definitely," Remi endorsed that assertion. "You belong here as much as I do. Now, it appears that Ivy does as well."

"Um, well… Steele's letting me stay here while I heal. There are some bad guys out to get me," Ivy admitted.

"It's more than that. Steele hasn't taken his eyes off you," Carlee pointed out.

Looking over her shoulder back at the magnetic figure, she found him focused on her. "Steele did save me. He's probably worried about what danger I can fall into here," Ivy finally said, settling on what seemed to be a safe answer.

"These guys save a lot of people. Steele's never brought anyone home. Does he think you're his Little girl?" Remi asked bluntly.

"You all talk about being a Little girl?" Ivy whispered.

"He knows you're his Little," Carlee affirmed, exchanging a look with Remi. "It's not a secret between us. We understand."

"You're Little, too?"

"I am. Definitely," Carlee assured her.

When Ivy looked at Remi, the other woman simply shrugged.

"She's a Little," Carlee corrected with a knowing look. "Steele's on his way. We'll talk more later. Let me point out a few people so he won't know what we were talking about."

By the time Steele reached her side, Ivy's head whirled with names. She looked up at Steele blankly. Immediately, he wrapped an arm around her waist and hugged her tight.

"Don't worry if you don't remember who everyone is. We'll slap nametags on our chests if we need to," Steele assured her.

The image of these rough guys walking around with "Hi, my name is" stuck to their broad chests made her burst out in tickled laughter. She leaned back against Steele for support as she enjoyed life—no bad guys threatening, no crappy bosses, no being alone. Ivy decided she was going to like it here.

When the others looked at her, she swatted her chest and forced out "Hi, my name is…" Steele still appeared confused by why that was funny, but the Littles got it immediately.

"Come on, Chuckles. Let's get you fed."

Taking her hand, he tugged her to the open kitchen where delicious-looking food tempted her, arranged beautifully in heated trays. Steele quickly washed the cup and lid still in his hand and dried it carefully, as Ivy looked around to see if anyone looked at her strangely. She only saw smiles. *They really do like Littles here.*

He picked up a plate and steered her to the first dish. "Eat all you want and go back for seconds."

"Who made all this?" Ivy asked, helping herself to some cut-up veggies to be healthy before scooping up a completely unhealthy, heaping spoonful of the cheesiest macaroni and cheese.

"We all take turns."

When she opened her mouth to volunteer, he cut her off before she could talk. "You're on inactive duty, Little girl."

"I could stir cupcake batter."

"Not for a few days," he decreed, lifting tongs to offer her some chicken tenders.

"Just one," she allowed, holding her plate out.

By the time they finished adding a bit of this and that, her plate was groaning under the weight. Steele plucked it out of her hands and carried it for her to a partially filled table. Placing the dishes in front of empty chairs, he introduced Ivy as he pulled out her chair.

After saying hello, Ivy let the conversations flow around her as Steele excused himself to grab their drinks. Checking out everyone in the room, Ivy noticed a man sitting by himself and wondered why he hadn't chosen to sit with the others. When Steele returned, he placed her lookalike cup in front of her. Suddenly thirsty, she lifted it and paused, staring at the sippy lid on top. Ivy peeked up at Steele.

"It's okay, Emerald Eyes. You won't have to worry about spilling anything," he reassured her quietly.

"Okay," she whispered, and lifted it to her lips experimentally.

"Chocolate milk," Ivy celebrated quietly and patted her Daddy's hard thigh.

Catching others looking at her, Ivy felt self-conscious. They were smiling her way, but being Little was so new for her. Trying to be subtle, she scooted closer to the dynamic man next to her. He didn't ask any questions, but pulled her chair tight against his. Steele wrapped an arm across the back of her seat and reassured her with caresses up and down her upper arm and shoulder.

In her sheltered spot, she observed those around her. These guys might look all growly and mean, but they laughed and enjoyed each other's company. It really was like a family. There was only one guy sitting isolated away from the others. Instantly, Ivy wondered why.

To her surprise, she saw Carlee approach the man with her meal to sit across from him. Carlee really was very sweet to make sure he wasn't alone. Curious, she tugged on Steele's vest to get his attention.

"Who's that with Carlee?" she asked, pointing to the couple.

With a look of surprise on his face, Steele answered, "Silver."

She could tell something was up by his expression. "You don't like him. He's the one you were talking about earlier."

"Like isn't necessary. I'm not sure I trust him," Steele answered.

"So, he's doesn't hold a position in the club?"

"He's the treasurer."

"That sounds like someone you should trust," Ivy suggested. "I could…"

"No numbers for you, Little girl. You're on medical leave. Don't worry about it. I don't have any reason to not trust him. Eat," he directed, nodding at her plate.

Obediently, Ivy scooped up a bite. When her immediate hunger eased, Ivy leaned against his support as exhaustion draped over her. Why was she always so tired? Without thinking, she took a bite of the delicious chicken when Steele held his fork to her lips. Realizing that she had allowed him to feed her, Ivy looked around self-consciously. No one reacted.

A few minutes later, he offered her a taste of a casserole she hadn't tried. It smelled wonderful. Opening her lips, she allowed him to place a small portion in her mouth.

"Mmm!"

"Good, huh? That's Remi's favorite. Have some more," he said to her quietly and held another bite to her lips.

When his plate was empty, Steele put hers on top of his. She let him feed her a bit more, but shook her head when her stomach was full. Ivy loved that he didn't pressure her but continued to offer bites every once in a while to make sure she hadn't changed her mind.

Watching him devour the rest of the food amazed her. Where did he put it? There wasn't a spare inch of flesh on his body to pinch.

When the conversation took a serious turn, Ivy listened carefully. The men seated around them began to give her tips for self-defense. Steele promised to give her lessons when she was fully healed, but for now, they shared vulnerable places for someone her size to hurt an attacker.

"Do you know how to punch someone, Ivy?" Kade asked, leaning forward.

Thinking it was a trick question, Ivy balled up her fist with her thumb protected inside her fingers. "Like this?"

"No, Little girl." Steele peeled her fingers apart to pull her thumb out. "You'll break your thumb that way."

"And it will be safe this way?" she asked, turning her fist around to look at it from different angles.

"Safer," Kade verified. "Something that doesn't take a lot of strength is to blind an attacker. Put your fingers together to form a spear and strike at their eyes."

Steele helped her form her fingers into the shape Kade suggested, and pulled her hand toward his face. Immediately, she tugged her hand away from him. She didn't want to hurt Steele.

"I don't think I want to know this," she whispered and hid her face against Steele's neck as she took hold of his cut to reassure herself.

"We want you to be safe, Ivy. If you're in trouble, don't hesitate. Strike hard," Kade growled.

"She's listening, Kade. It's just too much now. We'll practice when she feels better," Steele assured him as he stroked a reassuring hand over Ivy's back.

The men changed the conversation to focus on the repair shop, distracting her with funny stories about the customers. Ivy relaxed against Steele's brawny chest and listened to the dangerous men laugh about floofy dogs, entertaining customers, and messed-up tattoos. Exhaustion crashed over Ivy, and she yawned widely.

"Bedtime, Emerald Eyes," Steele announced as he stood to carry their dishes over to the kitchen where two members stood loading plates into the dishwasher.

Suddenly exhausted, when he returned, she wrapped her arms around his waist and leaned against him. Without saying a word, Steele lifted her as if she were as light as a feather to hold against his chest. Ivy rested her head on his shoulder as her feet looped around his waist. He swayed gently as he answered a few questions from the surrounding men.

In a few minutes, he walked back to his apartment. Setting her feet on the wooden plank floor in the bathroom, he put toothpaste on her brush and handed it to her before fixing his own. It felt strangely intimate to clean their teeth simultaneously. Somehow, this simple act made their relationship feel more real. Seeing a glob of foam on the corner of his lips, Ivy reached up to wipe it away and received a minty peck on her cheek as a reward.

When they finished, Steele washed her face and sent Ivy into the toilet area with a light swat on her bottom. After returning to his side and washing her hands, Ivy let him steer her into the bedroom. She was almost asleep on her feet. Somehow, she ended up tucked into the big bed with her teddy bear in her arms.

"Night night, Lucky."

As she tumbled into sleep, Ivy heard Steele comment on the name she'd settled on for her stuffie.

"Perfect name, Little girl."

CHAPTER EIGHT

So warm. Ivy rubbed her face against the lightly furry material. That didn't feel like Lucky's fur. *Hairy sheets?* She didn't remember those from yesterday. Blinking her eyes open, Ivy stared down into deep brown eyes that crinkled with amusement.

"Are you blowing your nose on me, Little girl?"

"No," she answered, horrified that he would even suspect that. His chuckles shook her body and only then did she realize she'd draped herself over his hard frame.

"Oh! I'm sorry." Ivy wiggled toward the side to slide off him, but Steele's hands spanned over her back, holding her in place. "Steele. Let go!"

"I like you here, Little girl. You fit perfectly." He flexed his hips upward slightly to press his thick erection against her.

"Oh!"

"I think you should call me something different now, Little girl," he reminded her.

"Daddy?" she guessed, still trying to figure out how to slide off.

"Exactly. I'm glad you agree," Steele said, finalizing their pact.

"Wait! You want me to call you Daddy… Like all the time?"

"Yes, Little girl. You've used it before, but now we'll make it official. There will be times you'll use my legal name because you want to avoid conflicts with others who wouldn't understand. Like at the bank, for example."

An image of her racing across the lobby with widespread arms, calling *Daddy*, flashed into her mind. "That would definitely not be appropriate if I want to keep my job."

"Probably not, but we don't need to worry about the bank now."

"I know I'm not irreplaceable, but they have to be scrambling without me to make the schedule and approve all the upper-level accounts." Her mind churned with all the small and big jobs she did every day. Who was taking all this on? The bank president was not the type of person to roll up his cuffs voluntarily to help.

"What's two hundred and forty-seven plus eleven hundred minus seventy-nine?" Steele asked.

The numbers rattled around in her brain, and what would have been ten seconds max for her to solve seemed insurmountable. "I don't know," she whispered. "How can I not know?"

His hand smoothed over her back as the other lifted to cup the uninjured side of her head. "You banged yourself up pretty badly, Little girl. You have to give yourself time to heal. That's why the doc doesn't want you to go back to work."

"I should have just stayed still in that dumpster and waited for them to come back and get me. I hurt myself for no reason."

"What do you think they would have done if all the Shadowridge Guardians would have been at their bikes when they returned? Would they have waltzed up to the dumpster and retrieved you or driven past, maybe trying again later? How many times would they have stopped back to get you?"

She looked at him and shook her head. Those guys would have given up on her quickly. Whatever they'd thought she could do for them, they wouldn't have risked getting caught—and they sure hadn't cared what happened to her.

"You were fucking brilliant to figure out a way to get people's attention and not lay there accepting your fate as someone's victim. You always fight back when your life is at risk. Even if you're hurt, you never give up."

"I'm not brave like you. I should have fought harder when they first attacked me. There wasn't much I could do tied up and wrapped in that bag."

"There were three of them and one of you. You survived to fight another day. I'm damn proud of you."

"You are? But I didn't escape. You had to save me."

"We can all use someone in our corner. I'm glad to have the Guardians behind me as well. I'm also glad to have one scrappy Little on my side."

"Thanks, Daddy." She deliberately used the name he preferred and loved the effect it had on Steele.

He cradled her head in one hand and turned their bodies to reverse their positions. Looking down to meet her gaze directly, Steele demanded, "Say it again."

"Yes, Daddy," Ivy said with a bit more ease. She enjoyed making Steele happy.

"Damn, Little girl. I was never going to let you go before, but now..."

"I'll have to go back to my real life some time, St... Um, Daddy." She made a face when she bobbled, using the right name.

"It will get more familiar, Ivy girl." He brushed the hair from her face tenderly to not touch her bruising. "We'll need to adjust a few things. You live on the other side of town."

"Yeah, it's a little quieter there. That's good after working in the hustle and bustle of the bank, but lonely at other times."

"Sounds like you need a companion," he suggested, raising his eyebrows suggestively.

She swallowed hard and admitted, "I don't know if my

neighbors are going to approve of a motorcycle gang boyfriend."

"First off, the Shadowridge Guardians are not a gang. We're a motorcycle club. We aren't thugs or criminals… Well, no one is now. Some have a shady past, but they've changed their priorities."

"But you all look like a gang," Ivy suggested.

"We look like a motorcycle club. I'll save an old lady's cat, fix someone else's kitchen sink, and change a teenager's tire. Then your snooty neighbors won't look down on my bike and tattoos."

"I don't mean there's anything wrong with you. I know you're a good guy. You just don't wear khakis and a button-down shirt." An image of his muscular body hiding under yards of fabric, with his tattoos peeking out, popped into her mind. *Yeah, he'd look good even in that.*

"Don't even consider it, Little girl. That's one thing that won't ever happen," Steele told her in a definite tone that brooked no argument.

'I could get a dog.'

"You're not replacing me with a fucking dog, Little girl."

"No! I didn't mean that!"

"That reassuring," he said with twitching lips, cluing Ivy in that he was trying not to laugh.

"Do you always stay here?" she asked.

"I do. We could live here. It's not fancy. I like to be here in case the club needs me."

"All your friends are here. It's safe."

"We'll stay here until they catch whoever targeted you. Then we'll make the tough decision."

"We'll stay together?" she asked, studying his face. Ivy didn't know how she knew he was the man she'd hoped to find. They just clicked together.

"I'm never letting you go, Little girl."

"Okay, Daddy. Wow! That does get easier," she marveled before adding, "Daddy? I have to pee."

"Go, Emerald Eyes. It's time to get up. Start thinking about how we can make love without rattling your head," he said, easing off and allowing Ivy to scoot off the mattress.

"Make love?" she echoed before squeezing her legs together and running for the bathroom.

By the time she and her red-hot cheeks emerged from the bathroom, Steele was already up and easing his jeans closed over his morning erection. That didn't help her blush at all. She froze in the doorway.

"Come on, big eyes. Let's get you dressed and grab some breakfast. Got anything you'd like to do while I work today?"

"I wish I had my phone," she mumbled, trying to say something as he stalked forward. The view of his bare chest just kept getting better with each step he took.

"No electronics."

"Maybe the doctor didn't mean for a full week. A glance couldn't hurt," she suggested.

"No electronics, Little girl."

His commanding tone made her bristle. "You know, you really don't get to make all the rules."

"The doctor set out that rule. I'm just enforcing it," Steele corrected as he halted in front of her. His gaze fixed on her face, and Ivy knew he watched her reaction closely.

"Fine. I'd like to go get my car today. I have an extra set of keys at my house. Maybe Carlee or Remi could take me over there."

"I'll drive you after work. There are still guys out there who threatened you. I'll call the police today to check on the progress of picking them up. Until they find them or I find them, you'll have a Shadowridge Guardian escort."

At the mere mention of the guys who had attacked her, Ivy's rebellion evaporated. "Surely they've given up now."

When he didn't answer, Ivy whispered, "Why did they target me?"

"I don't know, Little girl, but they made a huge mistake."

"Maybe I don't want my car," she said.

"It shouldn't sit in the parking lot. We'll go get it this evening and bring it to the compound."

"Okay."

"Let's get you dressed. As cute as you look in my shirt, I think you'll be more comfortable in a few more layers."

With no fuss, Steele helped her dress. When she was ready, he steered her into the bathroom and carefully brushed her hair. Ivy had avoided taming her wild tresses because of the bruising on one side of her head. Steele was patient and finessed all the snarls and tangles away.

"That feels so much better," she sighed gratefully.

"I'm glad. I won't braid it or put it into a ponytail like you usually wear it until your scalp is less sore."

"How do you know I usually wear a ponytail?"

"That's how you'd styled your hair before being wrapped in a sack."

"You are very observant," she wryly commented.

"Some people are that important. Let's go."

When she resisted, Steele turned to look at her. "What's wrong, Little girl?"

"I need something to do. I can't just hang around all day—I'll go batty."

"Let's stop at the play area. Maybe you'll find something there to help pass the time."

"There's a play area. You mean like for kids?" she asked skeptically.

"Don't knock it until you look. You can also learn how to work on a bike if you'd like. One of the guys will let you help them with a simple job."

"I'm not very mechanical."

"Faust will teach you," Steele assured her.

"Isn't he the guy that's always mad?" she asked nervously.

"He's a good guy. I can always depend on him. You can, too."

"O-Okay."

CHAPTER
NINE

Steele made a stop at an open area close to the kitchen. When he flipped the light on, Ivy's jaw dropped open as she stepped inside. There were books of different genres and types lining one wall. She spotted one section containing the paperbacks of a few books she recognized. Ivy had found those when she'd searched online for Daddies and Littles. But there were more she'd never seen. In addition, there were jigsaw puzzles to put together, board games, coloring books, and other activities.

"Choose a couple of things to take with you into the garage," Steele suggested. "You can always come back in and swap them."

Not wishing to rush to the books that really interested her, Ivy selected a book by a mystery writer she recognized. She also picked up a small paint-by-number kit. "Can I do this in the garage?"

"Of course. We'll find space for you at a table or the desk," Steele answered.

Holding her selections to her chest, Ivy eagerly followed him to the door that led to the garage. At the entrance, Steele fit the pink ear protectors she'd worn yesterday back over her head. She watched his lips carefully to understand what he said.

"Read or paint first?"

"Paint," she requested.

Within moments, he had her set up on the corner of the front desk. She watched people come in to drop off their bikes for repair. The variety of people who rode bikes—rough biker-looking guys to clean-cut executive types—intrigued Ivy. All were friendly and wished her a good morning.

When the second one asked her if she was alright, it dawned on Ivy that he was concerned about the extensive bruising on one side of her face. She quickly concocted a better answer, using a light-hearted response about an accident as an excuse. That seemed to satisfy everyone.

To her relief, no one recognized her from the bank. The bruising and her lack of makeup and business clothes proved to be a great disguise. That, plus she was in a repair shop. No one expected to see her there.

When the morning rush was over, all the guys dispersed around the garage, working on different cycles and tasks. Ivy worked diligently on her masterpiece, having great fun. She hadn't done one of these in a very long time. This break from all her hours at the bank seemed to illustrate how many things she'd stopped doing to dedicate herself to her job.

A flash of white made her look up, and she grasped the countertop to steady herself as the quick motion made her dizzy—not as bad as the day before, but disorienting. When she could focus, Ivy looked around to see what had caught her eye. A van drove by very slowly, creeping at such a remarkably unusual pace that it was still visible. Ivy froze in place. Hadn't Steele told her that her abductors had used a white van?

"Get down, Ivy," a deep voice demanded.

Ivy scooted off the stool she sat on and ducked behind the table. Peeking around the corner, she spotted a large man shift forward from the shadows of one bay to stand at the entrance.

His movements were panther-like, smooth and powerful, attesting to his athleticism and strength. The sunlight made his numerous tattoos come to life.

"What is it, Kade?" Steele asked, with his welding helmet in his hand.

Spotting the van, Steele raced toward the parking lot and yelled, "Fuck!" when it peeled away before he could even reach the front pavement.

"No way to get to a bike before it spotted us," Kade growled angrily. He stalked to the counter where Ivy crouched and wrote something down as Steele stalked toward her. "I got the license plate." Kade pulled out his phone and placed a call.

"You okay, Little girl?" Steele asked.

Ivy popped to her feet and wrapped her arms around his waist. "They were looking for me, weren't they?"

"Yes. Kade was watching the front."

"I didn't even notice," she whispered.

"You were in the shadows. It's likely they didn't see you. But if they did, they know you're under our protection now."

"Will they try to take me from here?" she asked as Kade approached with his phone.

"I've made the report. The plates were stolen from a car. I spotted two guys in front. One had brown hair and a slender build, the other, a big guy, was bald. Someone was in the back seat, but I didn't get a good look at him," Kade reported. "The police will monitor the area. I'll invoke a protection grid. Next time, we'll be ready. I'll move a couple of bikes up front."

"Thanks, Kade." Steele lifted one arm from around Ivy's body to shake Kade's hand before the man moved away.

Steele stroked his fingers over her hair. "It's okay, Ivy."

"They're not giving up. I thought maybe they'd decide I wasn't worth the risk, but they're not giving up!" she whispered furiously.

"It appears they will risk everything to get to you. Why? There's something going on that you haven't told me," Steele said, holding her chin firmly to keep their gazes locked together.

"What? No! There's nothing I haven't told you," Ivy assured him.

"Lying to your Daddy isn't a good idea," Steele warned.

"Steele!" Ivy hissed, her eyes darting to each side to make sure the other members weren't eavesdropping.

"They already know you're my Little girl, Ivy. Don't try to derail our conversation. What do they know? Do you have the passcodes for a billion-dollar account?"

"All that information is confidential, Steele. I can't tell you anything."

"To save your life, you'll have to. Whatever secrets you have, these guys will die to keep them safe. But you have to tell us what's going on. We're operating blind now."

Ivy swallowed hard. She focused on the front of his T-shirt and stiffened her spine with resolve. It was so hard not to divulge everything when looking in his eyes. She had to follow the bank's rules. "There are somethings I can't tell you," she repeated before offering. "I can go back to my house," she offered.

"It's that big, Little girl, that you'd risk tangling with the guys that might have left you to be crushed in the dumpster?"

"I don't know anything," she repeated stubbornly. Maybe if she said it enough times, he'd back down.

Steele shook his head in disbelief and let go of her chin. "Little girls should trust their Daddies to help. Let's get your painting stuff. We'll move you back to my area. I can get a light pointed on the table so you can paint there."

He picked up her painting and the small cup that held her paintbrush and water. Carrying them to the back, he set the items on his workbench to clear out a space on a small table against the wall. Within a few minutes, he had that spot illuminated and ready for her to work.

"I'm sorry, Daddy," she whispered.

"Having bad guys after you is not your fault. Failing to trust your Daddy with important information is. I'll give you some time to think before imposing a punishment," he answered with a look that told her he'd already thought of something that wouldn't harm her injury.

Not trusting her shaking hands to paint the correct small areas on her project, Ivy made sure all the paints were tightly capped before washing and drying the small brush. Crawling onto the cot Steele had set up for her yesterday, she sat leaning against the wall and opened the book she had selected. Two minutes in, her mind rebelled. She couldn't focus on all those mysterious details. Ivy thought about stretching out to take a nap, but she was still reeling from the van's appearance.

"You're welcome to visit the library again if that book isn't entertaining you," Steele called as he took a break from his task.

"I could watch TV?"

"No electronics. Go look in the playroom for something you're interested in."

"Alright. No electronics takes away a lot of options," she groused.

"It's only for a short time. Anything you want to tell me, Little girl?" he probed.

"Really… There's nothing for me to tell you." Ivy held his gaze, trying to hold a sincere expression.

His harrumph of displeasure clued her in that he didn't believe her.

"I'll go look for another book," she blurted.

"I like *Little Red's Visit to Grandpa*."

Ivy looked at him in complete shock. "You've read age play books?"

"Of course. I wanted to know what my Little girl has available to read. If something interests you particularly, perhaps there's something we need to experiment with together."

Her shock didn't dissipate. "You'll know all my fantasies," she whispered.

"There's nothing embarrassing between a Daddy and his Little girl."

"Do I get to know your fantasies?" she challenged.

"Oh, yeah."

The wolfish grin on his face made her bolt toward the back door of the garage area. The cooler outside air chilled her burning cheeks as she slowed to a walk to give herself time to recover before heading into the clubhouse. Letting herself in quietly, Ivy expected to visit the library without running into anyone.

To her surprise as she walked inside, Ivy spotted Kade inside instead of supervising everything in the shop. She'd already figured out he was in charge out there. Kade looked uncharacteristically relaxed as he leaned against a set of cabinets in the kitchen and drank from an oversized coffee mug. She remembered his name clearly. He'd calmly suggested she stab someone in the eye if she was attacked again. Ivy definitely couldn't forget him.

He was so focused on something that, curiously, Ivy followed his line of vision. Remi. He watched the cute Goth girl closely as she talked on the phone. Ivy smiled at the enchanting picture Remi made, twirling one of her low ponytails around her finger as she chatted.

What's going on with them? Ivy hid her grin as she crossed his path with a small wave before heading toward the library.

Running her finger over the spines of the books, Ivy scanned the titles, looking for the book Steele had recommended. Sliding it off the shelf, she flipped the book over to read the description on the back and felt her cheeks heat again. Could she read that with him watching? Ivy stiffened her back. She wasn't going to back down or let Steele know that his mere presence made the intimate relationship in the book sizzle even hotter.

Determined to keep her cool, Ivy stopped by the kitchen to get a chilled soft drink from the refrigerator. To her surprise, Kade appeared silently behind her and plucked the can from her fingers before she could open it. Without saying a word, he pulled out a small bottle of juice and cracked it open before handing it to her.

Swallowing hard as she looked into his stern face, Ivy whispered, "Thank you" before rushing to the door. Steele was tough-looking. Kade looked like he could rip the head off a bad guy and never blink. She peeked over her shoulder to find him looking at her. Feeling self-conscious, she lifted the bottle of juice like a toast to him. To her surprise, the ferocious-looking biker winked. Turning back to scurry through the door, Ivy grinned. She was discovering all these biker guys had a hidden soft side.

CHAPTER TEN

"It's just me, Little girl." Steele's voice wrapped around her before he slid his arms under her back and knees to scoop her from the cot.

Linking her hands behind his head, she melted against his chest as her Daddy carried her to the clubhouse. She didn't look up as he carried her through the crowd gathered inside for dinner directly to his apartment. Ivy should have felt self-conscious, but the combination of Steele's presence and the vibes put off by the group reassured her completely.

When Steele sat in an oversized chair with her cuddled on his lap, she sighed with delight. If only she could freeze this moment in time and never had to deal with life's challenges and all that seemed to be against her now. His hand stroked over her hair and returned to brush lightly over the bruising that was turning an ugly color of green.

"How's your head feel, Little girl?"

"It feels okay. The ache gets better every day. I don't get as dizzy when I turn my head quickly. I think I'll be okay to go back to work next week."

"Not happening," he firmly decreed.

"You're not really in control," she felt compelled to say,

correcting him. His amused chuckle told her Steele wasn't under the impression that she had any say in her recovery.

"You're not the boss of me," she reminded him.

"I'm your Daddy. There is no bigger authority out there, Ivy girl. The sooner you admit that to yourself, the happier you'll be. Are you hungry now, or would you like to take a bath and then have a light dinner before I tuck you in bed?"

"With bubbles?" popped out of her mouth before she could contain her excitement.

"I think I can find some bubbles for you, Little girl."

"Bath," she declared without allowing herself to let her embarrassment of being naked in front of him change her decision—besides, the bubbles he promised her would cover everything.

"Good choice," he agreed with a smile, and he hugged her before lifting her to stand between his legs. He stripped off the black leggings she'd worn that day and her pretty underwear.

"All the pairs you put in the drawer are the same color. Do you have any panties that aren't green?" he asked.

She shrugged and admitted, "It's kind of my thing. Most of my underwear is green. I think it brings me luck. And, with a name like Ivy, it's probably a good idea to like that color."

His hand cupped her face, and Steele told her, "Green has suddenly become my favorite color. Your eyes are stunning."

"They match my bruises," she joked, dismissing his compliment. There wasn't anything about her that was stunning.

"Stop." Steele pulled her T-shirt over her head and stripped off her bra, leaving her naked in front of him.

"Stop what?" she asked, feeling vulnerable as he looked over her body.

"Your eyes are stunning," he said, repeating the compliment she'd brushed off.

She stared at his serious expression. He really meant what he said. Steele wasn't giving her superficial compliments. "Thank you?"

"That's better. Let's get you in the bathtub." Scooping her up in his arms, Steele carried her to the bathroom and set her on her feet. "Go potty."

The urge to go hit her, and Ivy rushed toward the toilet as he turned to fill the tub with warm water. Enjoying the delicious view of his ass as he leaned over to check the temperature of the water coming from the spigot, Ivy pinched herself to make sure this wasn't a nightmare turned into a dream.

"Ouch!"

Steele whirled as he stood. In two steps, he was by her side. "What happened?"

"I was just making sure I was really awake," she mumbled.

He smoothed his hands over her shoulders before gathering her hair and securing it loosely with a large scrunchie. Steele guided her with a firm hand. "Let's get you in the tub, Little girl."

After urging her forward to the mass of fragrant bubbles, Steele turned off the faucet before helping her step safely into the tub and settle into the warm water. "It's perfect, Daddy," she whispered as she leaned back against the porcelain to close her eyes. Ivy sighed happily.

She peeked one eye open when she heard him moving. Steele knelt by the side of the tub, picked up a washcloth, and dipped it into the water.

"Keep your eyes closed, Little girl."

Steele stroked the cloth over her face before drying it carefully. The feel of something weighted settling across her eyelids startled Ivy. She froze in place. The netlike bag smelled heavenly and whatever it was pressed solidly over her forehead and eyes. She felt his lips drop a kiss on her hair before she heard him shift away.

In a few seconds, Ivy felt him stroke the washcloth over her feet and ankles. The terrycloth tickled between her toes, making her giggle.

Ivy considered suggesting that she could wash herself, but

pushed that out of her mind. He wanted to take care of her. Having him bathe her was exquisite. Unable to rely on her vision, her other senses took over. The sensations of the warm, fragrant liquid lapping around her, the silky bubbles clinging to her skin, and the brush of the cloth lulled her into an intimate bubble of space that only included Ivy and her Daddy.

"Spread your legs, Ivy girl," he directed, drawing the cloth over her inner thighs.

She held her breath, hoping he would stimulate her. The cloth simply whisked through her pink folds and washed her bottom. Disappointment crashed over her.

"Don't wrinkle your nose at me, Little girl. Keeping secrets from your Daddy does not earn you any playtime," he lectured as he washed her tummy.

"But I can't tell you stuff about the bank. They would fire me," she protested.

"I don't need to know all your business, Little girl. I only need to know what endangers you."

The cloth swirled over her breasts. Her nipples tightened so hard they ached. Ivy moaned when his thumb stroked over one tip, seemingly by accident. She concentrated, sending mental encouragement toward him to lavish her with caresses.

When he abandoned her sensitive peak and washed down one arm to her hand, Ivy pushed her lower lip out in a disgruntled pout. *That didn't work.*

"Who's in charge, Ivy?"

After a short pause to show Steele he didn't control everything, she admitted, "Daddy."

Steele ignored her small hesitation and continued to bathe her. Ivy allowed herself to be distracted as he washed each of her fingers, tugging them slightly and releasing the tension in her hands. *This is heaven.*

Finishing with her shoulders and neck, Steele massaged her muscles gently. He cupped her shoulder with one powerful hand

and squeezed gently. "Ready to get out of the tub, Ivy girl, or would you like to sit in here for a while?"

"Can I stay here? Just for a little bit?" she whispered.

"Of course."

Ivy listened to him move around the room as she relaxed. She loved how safe being with Steele felt. Holding her breath, she sent a wish into the universe, hoping to feel this way forever.

By the time they made it to dinner, most people had already eaten. The club members had dispersed through the room, playing pool, talking smack, and drinking beer. Everyone greeted and talked to them as they passed through the room.

Ivy was surprised these rough-looking guys had accepted her so readily. When they sat down at a table to enjoy the chili from the immense slow cooker, Ivy bumped her shoulder against her Daddy's.

"You okay, Little girl?"

"Your guys are so nice."

"You're one of us now, Little girl." He held a spoonful of chili to her lips.

As she chewed, a feeling of security settled around her. Even before all this mess, she'd missed having friends she could count on. Her job at the bank required that she interacted with the other employees with a bit of distance between them. She definitely didn't have any people she would consider true friends.

Ivy looked over at Carlee as she hung out with some of the club members. Carlee didn't know her at all, but she'd brought Ivy clothes to the hospital so she'd have something to go home in. Other than the bank president, no one she'd worked with for years had even visited.

"You're thinking too hard, Ivy," Steele warned and offered

her another bite, which she accepted to give herself time to concoct a response that he'd understand.

Finally, Ivy swallowed and admitted, "Your friends have my back so much more than anyone else in my life."

"I'm sorry, Little girl. It shouldn't be that way, but things are different for you now. The Guardians protect everyone who needs us in Shadowridge. You, however, are special."

"Because I'm yours?"

"Because you're mine."

CHAPTER
ELEVEN

During the next few days, the police returned her purse containing her dead phone. Seeing her keys and untouched wallet nestled inside made Ivy breathe a sigh of relief before shivering as she remembered having it knocked out of her hand as they shoved her against the wall. They hadn't cared at all about anything other than capturing her.

"Let's go get your car, Ivy."

"I don't know if I can drive," she said hesitantly.

"I'll be right there with you. Storm? Can you drop us off at the bank?" Steele asked.

"Take your truck?" Storm asked, straightening up from the chopper he was working on.

"That would be best."

"I don't want to bother you," Ivy apologized.

"No problem. We all have each other's backs here," the heavily tattooed guy pointed out.

"That must be nice," Ivy commented as the trio walked toward a battered truck in the parking lot.

It looked like it had gone through a million battles and barely survived, but when Storm turned the key, it purred like an expensive sports car. The look on her face must have been pure amazement as she glanced back and forth between them because both men chuckled as Steele wrapped an arm around her shoulders and hugged her close.

"Many things are much different under the hood than they appear on the surface," Steele said with a wink.

Ivy cuddled against him, telling herself she was giving Storm room to maneuver as he drove. The two large bodies staked a large portion of the bench seat, making her feel protected. She felt invincible between them even as they drew closer to the bank.

When her head swam from the motion of the curves, Steele helped her shift to drape over his lap, so his bulk supported her head as well and didn't move. His hand stroked over her back to comfort her as she relaxed, savoring the contact with his warmth.

"Last turn, Little girl. You can sit up." Steele assisted her as she rose from her position.

Smiling at the sight of her car waiting for her, Ivy was happy to have a bit of normalcy in her life.

Storm parked in front of the sedan and Steele hopped out and turned to help Ivy slide off the high seat. She automatically looked toward the large plate-glass window in the back of the bank and noted several familiar faces assisting patrons visiting the drive-thru. She raised a hand to wave, but no one responded.

In her mind, Ivy made a bunch of excuses for their lack of acknowledgement. Maybe they'd been slammed with bank traffic earlier or the glare through the glass didn't allow them to recognize her.

Steele wrapped his arm around her as if he felt her distress. "It's okay, Little girl."

"They aren't even looking at me," she whispered.

"Do you want to start the car before I leave, just in case?" Storm asked from his seat in the idling truck.

"It will be fine. Go ahead," Steele answered and closed the door.

Storm nodded and headed out.

"I think we need to go into the bank," Steele proposed, watching her face.

"I don't know if I can go in there," Ivy protested, moving closer to him as she turned away from the back entrance where those horrid men had kidnapped her.

"What's going to be easier when you return to work—going back for the first time alone or having me with you now?"

"You," she whispered.

"I have some checks to deposit. Come with me while I take care of business."

Taking her hand, Steele led her around the building to the front entrance. She caught sight of her reflection in the window. Her jeans and T-shirt were not the perfectly pressed suit that had become her work uniform throughout the years.

She dragged him to a stop. "I'm not dressed right to go in there. I could just wait by the car."

"You're not leaving my sight, Little girl. Do you really think everyone believes you wake up in those formal clothes? Someone has seen you in jeans before."

A few random encounters with bank employees outside of work popped into her mind. They knew she wore other things. She looked back at her image and grimaced at the large vivid green-and-purple bruising on the side of her face, wishing for makeup to disguise the damage she'd suffered.

Her gaze flew to meet his when Steele wrapped her fingers around the frayed vest he wore. She latched onto it with a fierce grip that made her knuckles white. Instantly, her anxiety diminished and Ivy's shoulders lowered from a stressed position around her ears. She nodded at Steele to let him know she was ready.

As they walked into the lobby, Ivy paused to look around. The familiar feel of the financial institution calmed her further, but she didn't let go of his cut.

"Ivy?" The woman at the front desk rose and rushed over to

stand in front of her. Her hand lifted as if her first impulse was to touch the bruising staining her boss's face before she caught herself and dropped her hand to her side.

"Hi, Virginia. I'm afraid the doctor hasn't released me to come back yet. Steele had some banking business to do, so I came to pick up my car," Ivy explained.

"The doctor? Mr. Harris told us you were on vacation," Virginia whispered.

"On vacation? No!" Ivy shook her head and swayed when a rush of dizziness swooped over her. Steele wrapped an arm around her waist to steady her.

Squaring her shoulders, Virginia glared at the tattooed biker and asked her boss, "Do you need me to call the police, Ivy?"

Not understanding why she'd ask that, Ivy stared at Virginia.

"Ivy, I believe Virginia believes I injured you," Steele said in a bored tone that expressed that this was not the first time people had assumed he was a criminal—or a woman beater. The rigid tension in his body next to Ivy was the only indication of his indignation at being stereotyped so harshly.

"Oh, no!" Ivy looked from him to Virginia and repeated her vehement rebuttal of that assumption. "He saved me. Those guys that abducted me when I left the bank tied me up and threw me in a dumpster like garbage."

"Someone abducted you? From here?" Virginia covered her throat with one hand.

"I was in the hospital before Steele took me to the Shadowridge Guardians' compound," Ivy rushed to explain.

"The hospital? Ivy, we didn't know." She turned to look at the other employees, who watched their interaction closely as they worked. Virginia waved over a woman who hovered a few feet away. "Beatriz, a group of men attacked Ivy when she left the bank after closing."

"What?" The color leached out of the young woman's face. She rushed forward to hug Ivy. "Are you okay?"

Ivy tugged on Steele's cut, drawing their attention back to the man next to her. "This is Steele, ladies. He saved me."

Virginia straightened her spine and held a hand out to the handsome man next to Ivy. "Mr. Steele, thank you."

Steele shook her hand and repeated the gesture when Beatriz offered hers as well. "Ivy actually saved herself by making noise."

"And, in the process, caused a brain injury that has to heal. The doctor won't allow me to come back until I'm less scrambled," Ivy explained. "I don't know why Mr. Harris told you I was on vacation. Perhaps he didn't want everyone to be worried about their safety. That should be the focus now. Everyone should leave in groups. Could you spread the word for me?"

"Of course. They haven't caught the horrible men who hurt you?" Beatriz asked.

"Not yet," Ivy warned, peeking up at Steele, who squeezed her a little tighter before shifting Ivy slightly. She moved without asking any questions.

He leaned forward to say to her softly, "Don't move from this spot." When she nodded, he strolled to the window to complete his business and allow her to speak privately to the women as he kept her in view at all times.

"Are you safe with him?" Virginia asked.

"With Steele?" Ivy asked and laughed. "I'm safer than I've ever been."

"When are you coming back?" Beatriz asked.

"The doctor won't let me come back for another week. Then they'll check to see how my brain is healing." Ivy paused to wave a hand over her bruising. "I hate to leave everyone in a lurch, but my thought processes haven't settled back into place yet. I'd be a detriment here."

"People have been so mad. We're all working extra days and longer shifts. Mr. Harris said it was because you had demanded to take vacation time without notice," Virginia shared with gladiator-level rage etched on her face.

Ivy used all her business skills to not allow her anger to show as well. "I don't know why he would tell you this."

"Oh, we'll be sure to spread the word about *your vacation* as well," Beatriz assured her.

"Maintaining a professional atmosphere in the bank is more important than anything else. I do not wish to return to the bank to find a conduct violation report for you or anyone else." Ivy tried to squash the rumor mill process before it could catch fire.

Beatriz nodded to acknowledge the warning. "Got it, boss. I can't wait until you're back. It will give people hope that this crap is temporary." Daring to hug Ivy, she dashed off as the lines at the tellers' windows grew.

"Several people are talking about turning in their notice. We'll try to hold it together until you get back. Don't worry about us. Just heal," Virginia urged.

As the powerful biker returned to Ivy's side, Virginia added, "Mr. Steele, keep her safe."

"I'll guard her with my life," he promised, and there was no way to miss the truth of that solemn oath.

CHAPTER
TWELVE

Ivy allowed the anger brewing inside her to show on her face as Steele escorted her to her car. "I can't believe that…" her voice lowered to a hiss to preserve her professionalism, "*asshole* told everyone I went on vacation with no notice and required everyone to work overtime."

Automatically, she had headed for the driver's side of the car, but Steele turned her gently to walk around the vehicle to the passenger side. She continued to fume as he helped her into the car and fastened her seatbelt across her lap.

When he slid in next to her and closed the door, sealing them inside, Ivy exploded, "I should sue him for slander. No wonder everyone shunned my greetings. That obnoxious, manipulative man!"

"I think asshole is a perfect name for him," Steele agreed dryly.

"Right!" she said, turning abruptly in her seat before grabbing the console between them when the world spun around her.

Immediately, Steele's powerful arm shot out to pin her firmly against the upholstery. "Do not let him have power over you, Little girl. Your soldiers are already at work."

"What?"

"Calmly look at the window now," he instructed with a nod toward the drive-through area.

Ivy shifted her view slowly from his face to focus on the area he indicated. The teller on duty in the far right station leaned to the side to whisper something to the next employee as she waved to Ivy with a big smile. The word passed to each in the row. It was overwhelming to feel the emotional response of everyone who saw her reversed in seconds, but Ivy knew it had. She settled back against her seat and returned their greetings with a wave.

"Now, they know he's an asshole," Steele observed as he started the car.

"They already knew he was a jerk," Ivy corrected. "We all did. Now, they know they can't trust him any more than I have for several months."

"Want to tell me what's up with him?"

"No. It's all boring bank business. I'll take care of it when I get back to work."

"You don't have to do things alone now, Little girl," he reminded her as he drove from the parking space, heading back to the Shadowridge Guardians' complex.

"Thanks, Daddy." She closed her eyes and gave into the exhaustion the brief visit had caused.

A quick turn to the left woke her, and Ivy sat up. Steele might be a daring motorcycle guy, but he drove like a new parent with her in the car. "What's wrong?"

"I just turned on Main Street and will go two blocks to Lemon Avenue," Steele said into his phone before touching the screen to activate the speaker function. He set it in the cup holder before squeezing her thigh reassuringly. With his hands back on the steering wheel, Steele divided his attention between the windshield and his side mirror.

When she shifted to turn and peek between the seats, he barked, "Stay where you are, Little girl!"

"Is there a child in the car, Steele?" a calm voice inquired through the phone.

"There are two people in this vehicle—one adult male and one adult female," Steele answered with military precision. "The white panel van is still following us. License plate YRP 299. Check the report for the Ivy Jenkins abduction on…"

As he talked, Ivy remembered there was a side mirror. She leaned forward to see more clearly and froze. The blood in her veins felt like it had turned to ice. Ivy wrapped her arms around herself and sank back against the seat, her desire to hide urging her to slide onto the floorboards. She reached for the buckle of the seatbelt to release it.

"Stay there, Ivy. I don't want you to be bashed around."

Ivy swallowed hard and followed his instructions without argument. They were after her again, but this time, she had Steele. "Okay."

After several long seconds, the woman Ivy assumed was a 911 operator said, "Sir, are you sure these are the same men that abducted Ivy Jenkins?"

"There are three men in the van. A muscular bald man is driving. In the passenger seat is a male with brown hair. There is one more in the second row of seats. He appears tall with blond hair, but I can't see him clearly. I believe the first two match the description in the report."

"Because of a large accident on the north side of town, I don't have a car in the area to send. If the van makes any threatening moves, drive to the police station for assistance. It is two blocks away."

The air turned blue with his curses as Steele disconnected the call and placed another. She watched him glance into the rearview mirror and turn immediately to the right.

"Put your head on your lap and wrap your arms over your skull to protect yourself," he ordered as Storm answered the call.

"Car won't start?" Storm's amusement was palpable.

"There's a white van following us."

"Where are you?" Storm's tone morphed to sound hard and alert.

Steele gave him their approximate location as he changed lanes, and Storm's terse answer followed. "We'll be there."

After straightening the car from the next turn, he rubbed a hand over Ivy's shoulder as she lay folded out of view. "I'm sorry, Little girl."

"Can the Guardians help?" she asked in a muffled voice.

"Yes," he answered in a clipped voice that revealed his stress.

Continuing his avoidance and attempt to lose the van, Steele weaved through traffic and the roads he obviously knew like the back of his hand. When he slowed, she started to sit back up, but he held her in place. "Almost safe, Ivy."

The sunlight vanished from the interior of the car. Steele turned off the car and slid out rapidly. With no one to stop her, Ivy sat up and looked around. She was inside one of the motorcycle bays. Twisting in the seat, she looked behind and the seatbelt seized, following her sudden motion.

With a curse, she unfastened it and turned around to see a line of Guardians standing in a row at the entrance of the repair shop. Each was armed with a gun of varying forms. She tried to get out, but Steele had parked next to the wall so her door banged against the concrete, making her wince. There's no way she could fit through there.

Sending mean thoughts his way before she scrambled over the console into the driver's seat, Ivy remembered he'd saved her again and remorse crashed over her. She peeked out the door and saw a barricade of hard bodies separating her from the road. The throb of motors filled the air and wheels squealed on the pavement.

"They're running," a deep voice announced, and the tension visibly ebbed from the men in front of her.

"What's going on?" she asked.

Everyone shifted, moving their guns down to their sides as they turned around. Ivy saw Steele secure his handgun in the back waistband of his jeans.

"Do you always carry that?"

"Yes, Little girl. Let's get you inside," Steele answered evenly as he wrapped an arm around her while he dug a hand into his pocket to throw the closest man the key fob for her sedan.

"Wait! What's going on? What happened to the van?" Ivy dragged her feet, trying to look back at the others until Steele scooped her up in his arms and carried her out the back door.

"Little girl." Steele shook his head.

"What? I don't understand. The van was following us?"

Steele remained silent as he opened the door to the club-house. The chatter of the few people inside ceased completely for a couple of seconds as he stalked through with Ivy cradled to his hard body. Their talk revived behind them as they entered the hall to the apartments.

Ivy pushed at Steele's chest. "Let me down!"

He completely ignored her protest until he entered his space. Then Steele placed her feet on the floor and pulled her into his arms as his head lowered to capture her lips. The kiss set a fire within her instantly as he took absolute control of the exchange, stealing the breath from her lungs and the strength from her legs. Ivy curled her fingers into the fabric of his shirt and clung to his powerful form as the fierce kiss overtook her thoughts.

"No," popped from her mouth when he lifted his mouth to step slightly away from her. Ivy bit her bottom lip in anticipation when Steele ripped her T-shirt over her head.

Air wrapped around her breasts, making her shiver. The heated desire in his gaze as it meshed with hers made her squeeze her thighs together. Her need skyrocketed as Steele unfastened her pants and thrust her jeans to the floor. Within minutes, she sat naked on the bed as he stripped inches away from her.

Focusing on every inch of the chiseled man's flesh as it appeared, Ivy dismissed his move to set the gun into the nightstand drawer. Steele leaned forward to yank free the laces of his battered work boots before toeing them off and stepping out of his jeans and boxers.

Ivy traced every muscle and groove in his form with her gaze. Steele was so comfortable in his skin, she loved to look at him. He stalked forward like a jungle cat on the hunt. She shivered at the thought that she was his prey.

He wrapped a massive hand around the back of her head and drew her lips forward to meet his. Ivy expected a savage kiss, but his lips wooed hers, nibbling and tasting as he explored her mouth. Encircling his neck with her arms, Ivy arched her back to plaster herself to his body. His heat radiated to warm her as he hugged her to him with a supportive arm around her back.

Slowly, he lowered her to the surface of the bed. Supporting his weight on one muscled forearm, Steele nipped at her lips before gentling his kisses once again. Unable to lie still, Ivy rubbed her pelvis against his, fully engaged in the seduction he lavished on her. Her focus so complete, her breath came hard and fast when he released her mouth to press fiery kisses to her jaw and the sensitive column of her neck.

Her eyes closed in utter bliss as his touch explored her, teasing and tantalizing a trail of arousal down the length of her body. His kisses followed leisurely, as if Steele had all the time in the world to taste her. She'd never been the complete focus of anyone's attention. The world around them shrank to the edges of the bed that supported them as his mouth moved lower to taste the length of her collarbone.

Ivy threaded her fingers through his thick hair. Completely focused on the zings of pleasure his touch sent through her body, she squeezed her thighs together, feeling herself becoming wet and needy. "Please," she whispered as his mouth hovered over her breast. His heated breath radiated to warm her skin, building her anticipation with each fraction of a second he delayed. Arching her back, Ivy thrust her chest upward to press against his lips.

"Daddy's in charge, Little girl," he growled against her breast.

She shivered at the dominant command in his voice. "Yes, Daddy," she whispered before exhaling in relief and excitement when he captured her nipple between his lips and rolled it tenderly.

"More, Daddy," she begged and gasped as he nipped at the tight peak.

"Be careful what you ask for, Little girl."

He trailed kisses and caresses on her skin, stopping frequently to taste her as if he had all the time in the world. She couldn't wait for the next sensation as the anticipation grew inside her. When he moved between her thighs and settled on the floor, she held her breath. Would he kiss her there?

Steele hovered over the silky curls between her legs. She watched his nostrils flare as he inhaled deeply to savor her essence. The animalistic act carved itself into her mind. The passion etched on his face revealed how arousing he found her scent. Her embarrassment evaporated as he tugged her hips to the edge of the bed before lowering his lips to tease her.

Ivy shifted her thighs apart in a silent plea for him to taste her. Steele glided the tip of his tongue down the cleft of her pussy. His "mmm" of appreciation at her flavor deepened her desire, and she yielded without reservation when he pressed her thighs farther apart and sat back to study her.

"Damn, Ivy. You're beautiful." Each second he gazed at her built the anticipation of his next kiss.

When he finally lowered his mouth to her, Ivy trembled as sensations cascaded over her body. Steele explored her pink folds with his lips and tongue. When he sucked her clitoris into his mouth, a keening wail of delight seeped from her lips. When he pulled his mouth backward, maintaining the suction, those feelings magnified, becoming almost too much until he released her with a pop of suction.

Hovering on the edge of an orgasm, she protested and tried to raise her hips to chase it. Steele's hands tightened over her thighs, pinning her hips to the bed as he devoured her. She understood immediately that he was in control. Not her.

He thrust two callused fingers into her tight channel and she screamed as an orgasm crashed over her. When she thrashed her head to one side, he released one thigh and firmly gripped her throat below her jaw to hold her steady. The primal hold pushed her arousal higher than she'd ever flown before as he continued to devour her. When the sensations overwhelmed her, Ivy screamed with pleasure, the sound echoing in the room.

"Little girl," he groaned, rising to his knees between her legs. He pressed a wet kiss against her stomach. "Stay."

Ivy didn't move a fraction of an inch as she watched him reach for a sealed box, unseal it, and rip the packet open with his teeth. When he pulled out the protection, she giggled at the sight of the neon yellow rubber.

He winked at her. "Safety first, Little girl."

Laughter tumbled from her lips. How many sides were there to her Daddy? The vision of him gripping his thick shaft to roll the condom onto his cock wiped humor away from her mind, and Ivy bit her lip. Could she take him?

"It's okay, Ivy girl. Trust me?" he asked, holding her gaze.

"Yes," she squeaked.

"Good girl."

Steele rubbed his hands down her thighs and lifted one thigh over his shoulder. Fitting the broad head of his cock against her opening, he pushed forward gently, leaning forward to collar her throat once again to hold her head steady as his shaft stretched her. The pressure was breathtaking.

Tentatively, she tried to shift her head, and his hand tightened, warning her. He was totally in control. Being frightened didn't enter her mind, Ivy was so turned on. She sucked in a breath as Steele filled her. The pressure built inside her. Could she take all of him?

Steele tightened his hand around her throat, interrupting her anxious thoughts. Her body reacted to his dominance, relaxing her muscles around him. His gaze held hers captive, not allowing her to look away. So intimate, she felt he could see into her soul. Without warning, Steele surged forward, filling her completely. He paused for a moment to allow her to catch her breath.

"Move, damn it!" she demanded, unwilling to wait for the pleasure she knew awaited.

"Language, Little girl," he reprimanded sternly before granting her wish.

Taking care not to rock her too abruptly, Steele pressed into her body over and over. A sheen of perspiration glistened on his skin as he held himself under rigid control. Even as their bodies moved together, building the sensations inside her, Steele controlled her movements as he targeted the sensitive areas he'd discovered.

Tracing the muscles of his chest and abdomen, Ivy stared at his masculine beauty—the scars scattered here and there added menace to his look. Steele could snap her in half with his brutal strength. More turned on than ever before, Ivy caressed his hard body to return the delicious caresses he lavished on her.

Steele's skill pushed her into climaxes that blended together until she could do nothing other than feel. His fingers tightened on her throat and he quickened his thrusts. A climax burst over her and she contracted around his shaft, drawing a low groan from his lips and a surge forward as he emptied himself inside the condom.

A slow smile spread across her face as he draped himself over her. His hand still firmly supported her neck to protect her head. Ivy loved feeling his heartbeat against her chest. The attraction between them was compelling and fierce. She loved it.

Her eyes flashed open. *No. I love* him.

CHAPTER
THIRTEEN

"The assholes drove directly into the traffic gathered around the accident," Talon groused, shaking his head.

"That didn't make it easier for you to catch up with them?" Steele said, thrusting his hand through his hair in exasperation. How did these guys keep getting away?

"Sorry, Steele. The police freaked when we rolled up over the hill. One patrolman actually drew his weapon and pointed it at Rock," Kade growled. "Like we're the fucking Hell's Angels."

Instantly, Steele wheeled around to check out the older member seated at the table. "Rock, you okay?"

"Doc checked me out. My heart's as steady as a rock," the weathered biker boasted.

After looking Doc's way and receiving a nod of confirmation, Steele shook his head. "Some new guy fresh out of a police academy?"

"Three days on the job. Sorry, Steele."

"I want them off the street before Ivy goes back to work. She's got one more week left," Steele announced, looking around the table to meet every member's gaze.

"And have you deduced why they're after her, Sherlock?" Talon asked with a smirk.

"No. I'm working on that."

Talon raised one eyebrow and said nothing.

"Just wait until you find your Little girl, jackass," Steele suggested.

"Like there's a Little girl out there who'll choose him," Bear chuckled and threw his empty beer can at Talon when he flipped him off.

"Since we're all here, there are some things we need to discuss." Steele looked around the table and asked, "Where's Silver? I asked him to be prepared with a financial report."

"Not here. I saw him take off with Carlee a while ago."

Everyone turned to look at Rock. Steele could tell he struggled to control his expression. All the Guardians could interact with each other peacefully. There were some relationships that were cohesive and others not so much. The lack of connection that Silver, their treasurer, had with anyone concerned Steele. Rock had practically adopted his daughter's friend years ago. Remi and Carlee had hung around the clubhouse since they were small. It didn't take a rocket scientist to see that Rock didn't approve of Carlee with Silver.

"Where has Remi been lately?" Bear asked, leaning back in his chair until it groaned ominously from the stress of his bulk.

Rock shook his head. "Busy working at the bar, I guess. I keep holding my breath, waiting to see what guy sporting a ton of black eyeliner she ends up with."

Kade's abrupt movement captured Steele's attention as the Enforcer's head whipped up to zero in on Rock. "Is she serious about someone?"

The older member shook his head. "Not that I know."

"If we're finished discussing the love lives of everyone we know, let's focus back on Guardian business," Storm suggested. "I'm setting up patrols around our compound and the bank branch where Ivy works. I don't like these guys daring to come so close to our territory."

"They know the roads. It's someone from this area, but yet they dared to get close to the compound," Faust spit out in anger.

"Who else thinks they shit their pants when we were ready and waiting for them?" Talon scoffed with a smirk.

"Good point. I'll set the patrols a fair distance from the compound," Storm decided. "Meanwhile, Steele, you need to get to the bottom of why these guys are risking everything to get to Ivy."

"Spanking often convinces a Little to tell the truth," Talon suggested with a know-it-all grin.

"Like you have any recent experience, wiseass," Steele growled, before reminding him, "Remember, head injury. She'll tell me soon. Having them chase us was a wake-up call."

Steele stared around the table, meeting the gaze of each member. He trusted these men with his life, but Ivy was more important than he was. "I want them stopped any way it takes."

"Got it, Steele," Talon answered with a small upward nod.

The jokester of the club's relentless expression was completely out of character. Glancing around, Steele saw that unyielding determination reflected on everyone's face. The Shadowridge Guardians protected their town and, especially, their own.

Conducting the rest of the meeting quickly, Steele didn't waste time in ticking off the items on his list. As Steele followed the other members out of the conference room, he spotted Ivy sitting by the door immediately and headed her way.

"Little girl, I thought you were waiting in our room?" he asked, lifting her out of the wide leather seat and sitting back down with her cuddled on his lap. When she snuggled against his chest instead of scurrying to get away so the others didn't see her, he knew she was upset.

"What's up, sweetheart?"

"I grabbed my phone off the charger and went through the emails and messages." She shivered against him.

He didn't like how she pressed a hand to her temple. She'd given herself a headache. "You're not supposed to be on anything electronic, Little girl. I should have locked that phone up."

Ivy looked at him in horror. "That would have been tragic. They're making threats."

"Show me."

"Can you look?" she asked, handing him the phone without looking at the screen. "They're in the messages."

Holding the device behind her so the words wouldn't be in her view, Steele found a number of messages from the bank president that on the surface seemed cordial as they asked how she was feeling. He frowned at the underlying tone that contradicted his encouragement for her to take as much time off as she needed to heal.

He kept searching for something from anonymous sources. There.

> Send us your access codes and we'll leave you alone.

> You thought the dumpster was scary. Give us the codes now.

> Hiding from us at that bikers' compound is smart. We're done playing.

> The Guardians can't protect you 24/7/365.

> You have 48 hours before we start targeting others at the bank.

> 30 hours. Send the codes or someone will pay for your stubbornness.

Steele glanced at the time on the phone. Thirty hours would correspond with the end of the following workday. The employees would leave the bank around that time.

"What are these codes?" Steele asked.

Ivy abandoned her struggle to keep the confidential bank information from him. They weren't going to give up. Steele would need to know everything to help her figure out what to do. "The board set up a system of checks and balances to divide the access to certain accounts and information between the board president, the bank president, and the bank manager. The codes allow me to complete certain processes without approval from someone else."

"Bottom line—what could someone do if they had all the codes?"

"If they had all the codes? Everything: enter the building outside of regular hours, access the vault, transfer funds, withdraw money, search employee records, wipe away accounting records, and much more. My codes would allow them to do a third of those activities."

"Was there a reason they divided the access between three people?"

Ivy looked around the room to make sure no one was within hearing range. "Someone moved money from an account that had been inactive for a long period of time with no way to track it. We only knew about that case because an heir approached the bank with statements that showed the discrepancy," she explained.

"And the records were gone so there was no way to prove what had happened to it," Steele guessed.

"No. There was also no way to determine if someone had tampered with any other accounts, either. I have my suspicions about who took the money and was collecting data to support an allegation before I take it to the board."

"Could someone be after your notes?" Steele asked.

"I wouldn't think so. No one knows about them. And they

wouldn't need the codes for those. For the first time ever, I didn't follow the bank's protocol. It's not protected in the computer system. I disguised the information in a printed file comparing bank usage for different age groups. It's in my desk."

"Did anyone know you were playing detective?" He did not like the idea that Ivy could have placed herself directly in the line of danger.

"No. No one. At least I don't think so."

"So, they want access into the bank's electronic system for some reason," Steele said, trying to pull together the information they knew so it would make sense. "Do they need to be in the bank?"

"It would be easier. Using my computer with the access codes would streamline the process."

"What access do you have, Little girl?"

"I can't tell you. I can't tell anyone. They're going to hurt someone today," Ivy said, trying to blink away the tears filling her eyes.

"Little girl, I understand that there is official bank business you can't share with me. Nothing is worth your life or anyone else's. Call the two who have the other codes. Set up a meeting for tomorrow morning."

He watched her thoughts race across her face. Finally, she nodded and reached for her phone. Steele wrapped an arm around her waist to hold Ivy in place when she scooted to slide off his lap.

"I need to talk privately, Steele."

Reluctantly, he allowed her to move away. He watched her closely as she selected a number from her directory.

CHAPTER
FOURTEEN

"I'll be fast," Ivy assured Steele.

"I don't like you going in by yourself," he growled.

"The bad guys aren't in the bank," she assured him, crossing her fingers by her side so he didn't see. Mr. Harris wouldn't attack her in the bank. She was sure of it.

"Five minutes and then I'm coming in."

Ivy didn't answer, but opened the door. Straightening her traditional suit jacket, she walked to the entrance. She could feel the effects of her injury as she moved, thanking Steele for vetoing her usual heels for flats. Making a big scene in the parking lot by falling off stilettos would not have aided her attempts to get in and out quickly.

Waving at the employees as she walked to her office, Ivy was glad to see everyone greeted her warmly this time. Virginia and Beatriz had erased Mr. Harris's attempts to turn her into the reason for everyone's additional hours. After opening her file cabinet, Ivy pulled one folder out and turned to leave.

The door was in sight when Mr. Harris appeared next to her. He stopped her with a firm hand on her arm. "I thought you were out for two weeks for your… *injury*?"

Ivy bristled at his implication that she hadn't been hurt. "I am. No electronics for two weeks. I wanted to practice with data on paper, so I came to get a sample to work with."

"What's that?" Mr. Harris held his hand out for the folder.

"Oh, just some data about bank usage in different age ranges. Lots of numbers and statistics," Ivy answered, flipping through the pages. "It's an excellent test to see if my mind can handle pulling this information together."

He continued to extend his hand for the folder. Reluctantly, she handed the packet of papers to him. Ivy held her breath as he scanned several pages. "This is extensive data for simply bank usage," he observed when he looked back at Ivy.

"Definitely. I know Nations Bank has closed several branches around the state to lower staffing needs and replaced them with ATMs and phone support services. Looking at this data helps us know whether that would be a good move for us as well," she improvised, fighting the fogginess of her brain to satisfy his questions.

To her delight, he looked pleased and handed the folder back to her. "I'm intrigued by your conclusions. Let's meet next week and you can share your findings."

"Definitely, sir. If you'll excuse me, my head is throbbing again."

"Of course. Get yourself back to normal for next week," he directed as he turned to walk away.

Ivy walked as fast as her head would allow to the door. She waved at Virginia as she approached, but didn't stop to chat. Her five minutes were almost up, and Steele wouldn't hesitate to follow her. As she reached the door, it opened.

"I'm here. Sorry. I had to stop and talk." Ivy stepped outside and wrapped her hand under Steele's arm for stability. "Let's get to the car."

A few minutes later, she rested her head against the car seat and willed her thoughts to stop spinning around in her mind. Ivy closed her eyes to block out the bright sun and struggled to pull herself together. It was vital for her to hold it together at the next meeting. When Steele linked his fingers with hers, she clung to him, feeding on his strength.

"Mr. Harris isn't going to the meeting?" Steele observed, and she realized he must have seen the bank president when Steele opened the door.

"No. Not this meeting."

Steele started the car and drove toward the main bank branch. The board president had requested to meet there. Ivy had only walked inside the impressive institution a few times. It gave off such a vibe of old-world security and tradition that she couldn't imagine anything bad happening there.

"Who are you meeting with, Little girl?"

"Can I just tell you everything when this is over?" she asked, not opening her eyes.

"I don't like this, Ivy. I can't protect you once you're out of my view."

"I'll be fine. Hopefully, I get this fixed now and it will all be over." She squeezed his hand before adding, "Thank you, Daddy, for being here to support me and understanding that there are some things I have to do on my own."

"My mind can understand everything, but my heart is telling me to turn around and head back to the compound to keep you safe."

"Soon," she promised, opening her eyes to look over at him. "All I want is to be there now, too. We never talked about how we'll handle this when I'm healthy again."

"I know you will have time at the bank, but when you're off the clock, you're with me. At all times, you are my Little girl even when you have to be professional," he answered, simplifying everything.

"Are we going to keep living together?" she asked.

"Of course. We'll decide whether we want to be at the compound or at your house."

"Where do you want to be?"

"With you," he answered honestly as he pulled into the parking lot of the massive building.

Ivy stared at the massively built biker whose fierce outside hid a tender but completely stern Daddy inside. "I just want to be with you, too, Daddy."

"Then we work everything else out."

After backing the car into a parking spot with a wide view of the building and the entrance, Steele turned off the engine. As Ivy reached for the door release, he covered her thigh with one powerful hand, tethering her in place. "What floor are you going to, Ivy?"

"The third floor, Steele. Let me handle this. You promised."

"I won't come in unless you call me or I see trouble. Then all promises are void."

"Thank you, Daddy. It may take a while."

"I have nothing more pressing to take care of, Little girl."

He released her leg, and Ivy forced herself to leave the safe bubble that Steele always wrapped around her. Her head had recovered a lot from the tension rising from her conversation with Mr. Harris. She walked slowly as she calmed her racing heart with deep breaths. She could do this.

Stepping inside the elevator, Ivy forced herself to smile at a professionally dressed executive who joined her just before the doors closed. She tried to picture Steele dressed in the expensive suit this man wore so well and had to stifle a laugh. Steele would look amazing, but she could already imagine his annoyed scowl.

Getting off at the third floor, Ivy walked down the hall to the CEO's office and checked in with his administrative assistant before taking a seat in the lush outer space. She glanced at the clock several times as she waited, knowing that Steele bristled more with every minute that passed.

> I'm waiting to go into the meeting. Sorry for the delay.

Be safe.

"Ms. Jenkins. Mr. Morton will see you now," the administrative assistant announced and stood to open the door into the inner office.

Carrying the folder by her side, Ivy crossed her fingers, hoping everything would turn out well.

"Mr. Morton, thank you for meeting with me."

"Ms. Jenkins, may I call you Ivy?"

"Of course."

"Please call me Richard."

Ivy smiled. "Thank you, Richard."

She perched on the edge of the seat and waited until he sat and looked at her. "Since the disappearance of the money from that account, I've tried to be vigilant to anything that appeared out of the norm. You may be aware that I was abducted from the bank as I left about a week ago. They taped my mouth when I refused to turn over the codes they demanded. I feared for my life as I was bound and wrapped in a sack before the three attackers threw me into the dumpster of The Hangout. Had a member of the Shadowridge Guardians not investigated the banging coming from the dumpster, I could have ended up in a compactor truck and killed."

"I saw the police report. How are you feeling? I know the doctor wanted you to have time away from electronics for your brain to heal," Mr. Morton said with a concerned expression.

Something was off. His concern didn't reach his eyes. Hoping it was just her imagination, Ivy answered, "I am much better than immediately after the incident. It was terrifying, and I know I'll never forget being tormented."

"And your share of the codes is what got you attacked?"

"Since they continue to demand my codes, yes."

"That's concerning."

"It is. Let me share with you the information I've gathered." She opened the folder and placed the first sheet on his desk.

"Differences in bank usage among age groups? I don't understand…"

"I hid the information I found in this report. Look at the first line. Those are an account number. Would you type it into your computer and we'll look at it?"

Mr. Morton shook his head as if this were a crazy waste of time but turned to his computer and typed in the number. An account popped up with a balance of two hundred and forty-seven dollars. "What am I looking at, Ivy?"

"Leave that window open and open the account of the next set of numbers."

"Almost four million dollars."

"Look at the date."

When he looked up at her with a serious expression, she continued, "I can track the movement of money from inactive accounts like the one we found previously and this smaller one that originally held a bit over five thousand dollars into the multimillion-dollar account. Someone did it using one of the codes divided up between the three of us for access. It does not match with my codes."

"Is this code listed on this page?" Mr. Morton asked.

"It is the sample number of the survey listed about midway down the page."

She watched him trail a finger down the document until he reached that line. His finger froze there as he read the code. "Do you know whose code this is?"

"If it isn't yours, it must be Mr. Harris's. Would you like to start a conference call with him?"

"Not at the present." He brushed off that suggestion before requesting, "Tell me. I'm assuming this document has other account examples. Who else have you shared this information with?"

"There is only one other copy of that information. It is in the quarters of the president of the Shadowridge Guardians," Ivy shared.

"That is in violation of bank regulations."

"I have been abducted, thrown into a dumpster to be crushed, and chased by maniacs in a white van. To be honest, possibly breaking bank violations is the least of my worries. The file will remain untouched there as long as I am safe."

CHAPTER
FIFTEEN

F eeling his skin itch, Steele exited the car and walked to the back of the parking lot. He was missing something. As he turned the corner, he spotted a white van with the stolen plates almost hidden by a retaining wall. Dashing to the side, he checked inside for occupants and found it empty. The sight of duct tape and rope made his blood boil. Steele took a few precious seconds to slash the back tires. They wouldn't take her again. Shoving his knife back into his pocket, he pulled his phone out as he took off for the entrance.

"The van is here at the bank headquarters. Ivy's in trouble."

"She's on the third floor, Steele. In a corner office." Talon reported her location from the tracker Steele had placed in her pocket.

"We'll be in the parking lot in sixty seconds, Steele," Kade promised.

As Steele burst through the door, the guard stood up from the reception desk. "Whoa, sir. Do you have an appointment?"

"Call 911," Steele yelled as he barged past the man to push the button for the elevator.

"Stop right there," the guard demanded as Steele noticed it was stopped on the fifth floor. He couldn't wait for it.

"Where are the stairs?" he demanded.

"Sir, I'm calling the police." The guard stood with his hand on his gun.

"Do it! If I'm right, there are intruders on the third floor." Turning to look around, Steele spotted the stairwell and took off for the doorway at the end of the hall. The man could shoot him. Nothing was going to keep Steele from protecting his Little girl.

"Sir! Stop!" the guard called after him.

In a flash, Steele was through the door and pounding up the stairs. He heard the door slam shut and knew the guard had not followed him. Hopefully, he was calling the police. Moving at top speed, Steele reached the third floor and burst through the door into the hallway. Without waiting to debate which way to go, he ran down the hallway, looking for the large corner office.

"I'm glad you chose to bring me this information, Ivy. I will take care of it." Mr. Morton picked up his phone and typed in a brief message. Almost immediately, the doorway into what Ivy had assumed was a private storage area or executive bathroom opened.

Two men walked out. The large bald man smiled, making her blood chill in her veins. Immediately, she stood and backed toward the door into the corridor.

"Mr. Morton…" she started when the door behind her opened. A slender man with brown hair pushed a custodian's cart inside.

"Take care of her this time," the board president directed, meeting the latest arrival's gaze.

Trying to keep from whipping her head from one side to the other, Ivy knew she needed to keep herself from becoming dizzy. She fumbled for her phone and the man closest to her knocked the device from her fingers. Panic flared through her body at the thought of those men getting ahold of her again. She didn't even need to hear their voices to recognize who they were.

There were too many people in the building for them to get away with this. Ivy opened her mouth and screamed as loud as she could. The large man moved quickly to strike her with one gigantic fist in the middle of her chest, cutting off the sound of her cry for help abruptly. Ivy bent forward, struggling to regain her breath and control the pain while trying to find a safe spot. She heard her name bellowed in outrage and knew Steele was close.

Dropping to her knees, Ivy scrambled under a small table as the men surrounded her. One dragged her out by the hair, and through the tears filling her eyes, she saw Mr. Morton disappear out the side door the two men had entered from. Fury burst through her mind and Ivy reacted.

She thrust an arm toward her attacker, automatically balling her fist as Kade had taught her at dinner. The impact rattled her arm as she struck his eye. When he howled and turned away, Ivy launched herself toward the door. The largest attacker grabbed her arm, wrenching her shoulder as he gathered her hands behind her back. The half-blinded man slapped the tape in his hands over her mouth before she could shout. She struggled to land another blow, kicking when she couldn't free her arms. They had just pulled a zip tie tight around her wrists when the door burst open.

"Steele!" Ivy screamed against the tape sealing her lips closed. The large man holding her threw Ivy to the side as Steele barreled toward him with rage, twisting his face into a dangerous mask. She watched as Steele dropped the brute to his knees with one well-placed blow before turning to face the second man who rushed him.

"Get safe, Little girl!" Steele ordered in a tone she couldn't ignore no matter how frightened she was.

Scrambling to get out of the way, Ivy ducked under the table once again. She couldn't see well and trembled at the sound of blows being exchanged. *Please! Let Steele be okay!*

"Steele!" Kade's deep voice rang through the room, and Ivy scooted back farther. Help was here. Steele wasn't alone.

It was all over in a few minutes. Three men lay stretched out on the carpet with their hands fastened with the zip ties they had brought to secure her.

"You almost lost this one." Talon's amused tone made her peek out of her hideaway to see Mr. Morton with his immaculate clothes rumpled and torn, being pushed into the office. "He seemed to think this folder was important."

Steele's body appeared before her as he dropped to his knees. "Come out now, Little one. Let me make sure you're safe."

As she tried to scramble awkwardly into his arms with her hands secured behind her back, a loud voice filled the room, making Ivy freeze in place.

"Police! Everyone put their hands up."

Her Daddy slowly raised his arms as he stayed by her side. He refused to move as the police tried to straighten out what had happened here. When the police fished Ivy out, one look at her taped mouth and bound hands convinced them quickly who the bad guys were.

Watching Mr. Morton walked out to a squad car in handcuffs felt amazingly good. Ivy couldn't believe the man she'd chosen to be the good guy in this mess had actually turned out to be the embezzler.

She rolled her eyes as she realized Mr. Harris hadn't been behind this. Nevertheless, he had been a royal asshole. She didn't understand why he'd told everyone she'd been on vacation. Had he done so thinking he was protecting her privacy? She really needed to have words with him, and she would the next time she saw him.

"I saw that guy's eye. It's going to be one heck of a shiner," Kade mentioned as the Shadowridge Guardians stood gathered around her while the police escorted the three thugs who'd attacked Ivy and continued to threaten her from the building.

"I guess I had an excellent teacher?" Ivy whispered, unable to believe she'd remembered the few things the Enforcer had told her.

Steele hugged her close to him. He'd left her side only for a few minutes while giving his statement when the police insisted. The officers' demeanor changed when they found a record of the previous assault and Mr. Harris arrived to represent the bank. To Ivy's surprise, he vouched for her.

"Mr. Harris…"

"We will meet in my office at eight a.m. on the day your medical leave expires. I have already been in contact with the vice president of the board and have updated him. The tech department has frozen Mr. Morton's access and code authorities effective immediately. The board is holding an emergency meeting this afternoon."

"Do I need to be there?" Ivy asked, clinging to Steele's cut despite her attempts to look professional in front of her boss.

"No, Ivy. You've been placed in a very dangerous position, and the board knows they owe you for protecting the bank's assets. I'm guessing you met with Mr. Morton to share the evidence that you'd found."

"Yes," she admitted. "I'm afraid I thought it was you."

"I can understand that. I'll admit you were at the head of my list of suspects as well. It appears that Mr. Morton deceived everyone." He held out his hand for Ivy's. "I vote we let bygones be bygones and work together for the benefit of the bank."

"I'd love to start again," Ivy confirmed as she shook his hand.

When he excused himself, Ivy looked at Steele in amazement. He simply raised his eyebrows in a silent echo of her disbelief. "Ready to go home, Little girl?"

The view of the van being hauled away by the police made her happy. They wouldn't have to worry whether anyone was following her now.

She waved a hand at the departing tow truck. "I could go back to my house now, Steele. You don't have to protect me anymore."

"We could stay there tonight if you'd like to pick up more clothes," he agreed. "Daddies don't let their Little girls stray too far away. After the scare today, I don't think my heart could stand having you out of my arms tonight."

"Sir, we need to make sure they did not hurt the young lady," an ambulance driver requested.

"I'm okay," Ivy rushed to reassure the paramedic.

"It's no cost to have us double check your heart rate and make sure you didn't re-injure yourself, miss. I understand you're recovering from a head injury."

She looked at Steele, silently requesting his help to get out of this. She smiled when he assured the paramedic, "We have our own medic. He'll check her out and make sure she's okay."

"You'll make sure someone with training examines her?"

"Definitely. I'll be the first to bring her in if there's a problem."

When the man nodded and turned to head back to the ambulance, Ivy tugged on Steele's vest. "Thanks. I've had enough for the day."

"Oh, Doc's going to check on you. He takes care of everything for us," Steele assured her.

She grinned at him happily. Anything was better than going back to the hospital or getting in that emergency vehicle.

CHAPTER
SIXTEEN

"Hi, Ivy. How do you feel?" Doc asked quietly before sitting on the couch next to her.

"I'm good. I don't know why Steele insists on you checking on me," Ivy said quickly. She'd hidden her teddy behind her when Doc had entered Steele's apartment.

"You're injured and we need to make sure you didn't hurt yourself worse," Doc answered, nodding at Steele. "He's a worrywart."

Ivy stared at him, trying not to laugh at the accusation that her tough Daddy worried about anything. Steele's chuckle made her look at him quickly, jostling her head. "Ooh!" she gasped and set her hand down on the cushion to ground herself when the world spun around her.

When everything settled back into place, she looked at Doc and said, "Maybe it isn't a bad idea, but that happened when I moved my head too fast before today."

"Gotcha. Let me look at your eyes first, Little girl." Doc shifted to kneel on one leg before her so their eyes were on the same level. He opened a small satchel and pulled out a penlight.

"Look at my nose. Good girl. Now, follow the light with your eyes." He held a hand over her left eye and then her right as he tested her responses.

"How's the head? Do you have a headache?" he asked as he turned off the light.

"Shining a bright light in my eyes didn't help," she muttered unhappily.

"I'll take that as a yes, your head hurts. Steele, get her a couple of those over-the-counter pain tablets, please."

"I thought you didn't have a headache, Little girl," Steele said ominously as he shook out the pills.

"It wasn't bad until Mr. Spotlight came in to torture me," she groused, knowing she was already in trouble.

"No torture, Ivy. It is important that you tell me the truth," Doc warned as Steele handed her an open bottle of water and the medicine.

Popping the tablets into her mouth, she washed them down with a gulp of water. She grimaced at the feeling. It felt like she was swallowing boulders. When she saw their worried expressions, she forced herself to say, "I guess you want to know my throat hurts, too."

"Definitely. Inside or out?"

"Both. They tried to yank me out into the open by my hair and my neck got twisted around. Even though I couldn't make a ruckus, I kept screaming. I think I irritated everything inside, too," she admitted.

"Let me check." Doc pressed several places on her cervical spine as he observed her reaction. None of that felt painful until he stroked over the front of her throat.

"Ouch!" she complained.

"Sorry, Little girl. There's some soft tissue damage to your neck. Steele, keep an eye on her if she frequently rubs the back of her neck or if the pain increases, she'll need an x-ray."

When Steele nodded, Doc requested, "Open your mouth, Ivy. Let me see inside, too." He cupped her chin and held the flashlight expectantly.

"Ahh!" she said after opening her mouth.

"Definitely red. Could be from screaming, might be something else. Any time you're under stress like you have been, your entire immune system is being attacked. I'm going to give you a quick exam to make sure you haven't caught a bug."

Doc pulled a stethoscope from his bag and fitted it to his ears before holding the bell of the device to her chest and back as he asked Ivy to take a few deep breaths. "Sounds good. I don't hear any rumbles in your lungs. Let's get a quick temperature to make sure you're not running a fever."

Replacing the stethoscope in his bag, Doc pulled out a small package of supplies. "Steele, this is the starter pack I've decided all the Daddies need. I'll let you explore through everything I've included. If you need refills or something in addition, let me know."

He opened the small case and Ivy peered inside to see what looked like a regular first aid kit. What he pulled out was not something she expected to see.

"What's that? A thermometer for an elephant?" Ivy trumpeted like one of the giant pachyderms to make a joke of it. Instantly, she grabbed her throat and croaked, "Bad idea."

"Definitely," Doc sympathized. He set the thick glass tube to the side and removed a tub of lubricant. Opening the jar, he set it next to the first item.

"Let's get your leggings off, Little girl."

"My pants? Why?" She looked at him suspiciously.

"So I can take your temperature," Doc explained easily.

Finally, everything clicked into place in her mind. "You think you're going to put that in my bottom?"

"Either I am or your Daddy is," Doc answered.

Ivy started to shake her head in denial, but Doc cradled her head between his hands, stopping her. "No sudden movements."

"Daddy it is," Steele said firmly. He picked up Ivy from the couch and rotated her body slowly so he didn't discombobulate her brain as he sat down. She clutched at his calves, finding herself over his lap. Pressing one hand firmly against the middle of her back, he pulled her panties and leggings halfway down her thighs.

Cool air rushed over her skin, making Ivy shiver. Reaching back, she grabbed the bottom of his vest and tugged it. "Daddy?"

"It's okay, Little girl. I'm going to take care of you. You're safe with me and Doc. Let us check that you're feeling okay." Steele rubbed his hand over her lower back and over the swell of her buttocks.

Ivy risked a look up at Doc. He wasn't even looking at her butt. Doc had picked up the lubricant and was dipping the end into the thick mixture. When he lifted his head and their gazes met, he reassured her, "Little girls need special treatment from their Daddies. I'm just here to assess you medically."

She couldn't help but notice that as they talked, he passed the thermometer to the man holding her firmly in place. With a gigantic sigh, Ivy lowered her head to dangle over her Daddy's lap. *At least I'm not getting spanked.*

"Good girl," Steele praised before spreading her bottom to reveal the small, tight opening hidden between her cheeks.

The rounded tip pressed against the ring of muscles and slid easily inside her body. The lubricant made it impossible for her to keep it out by tightening her muscles. Steele pressed it inside until it stopped, poking her a bit. The rod was cold and seemed to radiate through the walls of her channel.

"Little girls sometimes try to keep their Daddies from placing the thermometer fully in their bottoms. Twist the end slightly as you press in. You may find that she hasn't allowed it to enter completely," Doc counseled.

Ivy wrinkled her nose and snorted her displeasure as Steele pressed the thick device deeper inside her. "Doc knows your tricks, Ivy."

"I feel sorry for his Little girl," she grouched.

"I haven't been lucky enough to find my Little girl, Ivy. I hope I will soon," Doc shared.

"Lucky!" Ivy whined, reaching with one hand for her teddy bear who had fallen off the couch as Steele moved her.

"Doc, would you get the stuffie who tumbled off the couch? That's Lucky." Steele rubbed her back once again with one hand while the other lay against her buttocks, holding the device inside.

"Of course."

She saw his feet appear in front of her. Doc squatted easily at her side and held the stuffie for her to grab. "Lucky is a very fortunate bear to have ended up in the arms of a Little."

Eager to think of anything other than the thermometer in her bottom, Ivy kissed Lucky before hugging him to her chest. Curious, she asked, "Why is it better to be the stuffie of a Little girl?"

"Lucky won't be a toy that is forgotten. He'll never sit on a shelf and get dusty. I would bet five years from now you'll still kiss his left ear."

"I don't always kiss his left ear," Ivy denied as Doc stood back up to lounge against the wall as he observed her treatment.

"You do. Then you hug him tight," Steele corrected her gently.

"Is it time for that thing to come out?" Ivy asked, feeling self-conscious that her Daddy had watched her cuddle with her bear when she thought he was busy.

"Not yet. Two more minutes. I'd carried Lucky around in my saddlebag on my bike for several months. He was lonely and needed a friend," Steele admitted.

"Do all the Shadowridge Guardians have teddy bears on their bikes?"

"They do. We carry them to give to anyone who needs a stuffie to love them—kids, adults, and Littles," Steele explained.

A quiet beeping sounded in the room. Immediately, Steele removed the thermometer and checked her temperature. "Two tenths of a degree above normal, Doc."

"The slight fever indicates it's most likely a virus and she'll rebound quickly with rest and fluids. I have a feeling all the stress put Ivy at risk of picking up a bug easily while in a crowd. You'll have to monitor her, Steele, to make sure it doesn't rise any higher."

"Will do, Doc. Naps and push juices?"

"Chilled fresh fruit and lots of water are even better than juice. You can even combine the two and slice something like strawberries or watermelon into her water to flavor it," Doc suggested. "The pack here has some pain-relieving suppositories if Ivy's head hurts and she's not eating. Those have the benefit of lulling a Little who's in pain but refuses to take a nap."

"Suppositories? Like to go in my bottom?" Ivy asked in disbelief.

"Yes, Ivy. They prevent stomach problems when repeatedly taking pain medication. Is your head better now after taking the tablets?" Doc asked.

"I don't need any more medicine," she rushed to assure him.

Steele's and Doc's gazes meshed and Steele nodded his agreement of whatever silent message the two shared. Ivy swallowed hard. She had no doubt that the next time she complained about having a headache he would try the new type of medicine. Quickly, she spoke to make sure they didn't dose her today.

"I feel a ton better now."

"Good. I'm glad to hear that. Steele, let me know if you have any concerns or Ivy doesn't feel better in the next few days," Doc said, pushing away from the wall and heading to the door.

When the door closed behind him, Ivy struggled to move off Steele's lap. *Smack!* She froze in place as the sharp swat stung her bare bottom. A second and third followed quickly, spreading the sensation on her skin. Instant arousal flared inside her, and Ivy squeezed her thighs together, trying to stop the juices gathering between her legs.

He can't know that spanking turns me on!

That punishing hand rubbed over her bottom. She hoped he wouldn't discover her reaction.

"Little girls need to be spanked, Ivy. When your head heals completely, I'll spank you as punishment, as well as for pleasure."

"For pleasure? That's just twisted," she protested. "Can I get up now?"

"No, Little girl. Spread your legs."

Ivy wanted to shake her head but forced herself to stop. She'd gotten so dizzy too many times. She simply tugged wordlessly on his cut, asking for him to understand.

"I know you don't want to, Ivy. I've asked you to follow my directions," he said ominously.

"No."

"You have earned a consequence, Little girl."

"You can't spank me," she taunted with fake bravado.

"It's not necessary this time."

Steele gathered her easily into his arms and stood. His strength controlled her attempts to free herself as he walked into the bedroom. Carrying her as if her weight didn't tax him in the least, Steele strolled into the bedroom and placed her across the bed on her back. Before she could react, he grabbed the leggings bunched around her ankles in one hand and twisted the material to trap her legs together. Using her pants as a handle, Steele pulled her legs up and back over her torso, pinning Ivy's body to the soft comforter and lifting her bottom. Grabbing his pillow, Steele placed it under her hips, elevating her body on an angle.

"What are you going to do?" she asked, hugging Lucky to her chest.

"As you pointed out, I can't spank you, yet. There are other ways your Daddy can make sure you pay attention to what he asks you to do." Steele lowered his hold on her ankles. He stripped off her leggings to bend her legs and spread her thighs wide.

Totally exposed to his view, Ivy tried to struggle, but he'd trapped her in such a way that she couldn't thrash around. She looked up at Steele, ready to plead for him to let her go, and found him staring at her most intimate places. His gaze focused on her.

"I'm going to enjoy this as much as you do, Little girl," he growled as he shifted his stiffening cock in his jeans.

"Is it too late for a warning?" she whispered.

"Way too late, Ivy. I'll show you what happens to Little girls who don't follow their Daddy's instructions." He paused for a few long seconds to look at her. Each moment made her wetter until she felt drenched.

Finally, he moved. Ivy exhaled the breath caught in her throat. When he pulled out a device with a rounded head, she reversed the process and inhaled sharply. *Is that a vibrator?* She stared at it as he set it on the comforter in her view.

Quickly, she pulled Lucky over her eyes to hide her heated face from him. Another rustle in the drawer made her peek under the teddy's soft fur. A slim purple wand joined the larger one.

"Lucky for us, your bottom is already lubricated."

"What?" she gasped, automatically squeezing her buttocks together to feel the slippery lubricant that still clung to her skin. Ivy pulled Lucky back to her chest so she could send a pleading look to him.

Steele ignored her question as he picked up the small device and pushed the flange on the end through several distinct patterns of vibration. Even feet away from her body, Ivy felt like she could feel each one.

"I wonder which you would like the best?"

When she didn't answer, he settled on a soft, steady hum. "We'll have to experiment. Tell me how you like this one."

After placing the rounded tip at her exposed puckered opening, Steele pressed it gradually into her bottom. Thicker than the icy glass thermometer, this buzzing vibrator activated every nerve in the tight passage. She clenched her teeth as the novelty of play in this *naughty* area immediately turned up her arousal.

Ivy looked up at Steele, not knowing what to say. Squeezing her ankles tighter for a second, he watched her with a stern expression that commanded her obedience.

"I'm sorry, Daddy," she assured him.

"Thank you, Little girl. I'm glad you're learning your lesson. We're not done here yet."

She watched as he picked up the larger wand and pressed a switch on the side. Ivy could hear the powerful vibration. Swallowing hard, she waited for her Daddy's next move.

He glided the vibrator down the inside of her right thigh, passing over her needy pussy so closely she could sense the hum before he ran the device up the inside of her left.

"Naughty Little girls get teased," he said softly as he repeated the motion, only this time, the hum glanced over her mound.

"Daddy!" she begged. The buzz in her bottom seemed to vibrate through her body. It set all the nerves in that area on fire but wasn't enough to make her come. *At least, not yet.*

"What's going to happen the next time I ask you to do something?"

"I'll do it," she promised, fusing her gaze with him to convince Steele she was telling the truth.

"That's my good girl. I think you deserve a treat for learning such a big lesson."

Steele pressed the rounded head of the vibrator fully against her. The strong pulsation ricocheted through her body. Ivy teetered on the edge for a split second before her body responded with a massive wave of pleasure. As it crashed over her, she couldn't keep a scream from bursting through her lips. She sagged on the comforter when Steele lifted the device away.

"That setting works. Let's try this one," Steele suggested, pressing the end of the implanted device so the buzzing pattern changed. "Let's call this option two."

Watching him bring that broad head close once again, Ivy begged, "Can't that be enough? I've learned my lesson."

"Daddy's in charge of your punishment, Ivy. He's in control."

The pulse filled her senses, and she held on to Lucky as he brought the larger one closer. This time, she held out for a few seconds before another climax exploded inside her. She panted as he moved the vibrator away.

When his hand moved lower to change the setting of the small vibrator, Ivy asked, "How many settings are there?"

"Seven, Little girl. Here's number three. Tell Daddy what you think."

Her scream of pleasure followed, answering all his questions. She felt wetness jet from her body and babbled, "I'm sorry. I didn't mean to go," thinking she had peed.

"You're a perfect, good Little girl, Ivy. I'm so glad you're enjoying your lesson. Squirting shows me this pattern is your favorite so far. Let's see if we can find another one that pleasures you so completely." After switching to the next style, Steele leaned forward to capture her lips roughly. His fierce look of passion revealed just how much her display affected him.

So overwhelmed by the sensations coursing through her, Ivy felt herself beginning to float in her mind. She could concentrate only on her Daddy and the way he coaxed her body to feel so many things. Ivy hadn't known this level of bliss existed. Her Daddy was in charge and she loved it.

When he revealed the final vibrator pattern, Ivy panted. At the feel of his hand spreading over her bruised throat, squeezing firmly to tether her in place, her body burst into an earth-shattering climax. As grayness hovered on the edges of her vision while he controlled her breath, Ivy sizzled inside. She was completely unafraid and savoring his skilled finesse. The sensations were more than she would have thought possible. When she struggled to control her breathing, his hand eased, allowing the air to gush into her lungs. She understood he deliberately replaced the scary memory with one filled with so much pleasure.

The vibrator eased from her body, and she melted onto the mattress. Through hooded eyes, Ivy watched Steele turn off the large wand by pressing the end one more time to silence the device. She knew she was bad when she hoped he'd repeat the treatment again soon. Her fingers crossed almost on their own.

"Close your eyes, Little girl," he instructed as he lowered her legs to rest on the bed as well.

She followed his instructions without hesitation and felt him turn the vacant side of the comforter over to cover her. Her body still buzzed with the delight he'd lavished on her. Her mind escaped into sleep, leaving everything in Steele's hands.

Just the way he wants it.

CHAPTER
SEVENTEEN

The next week went by in a blur. To say she got used to having her temperature taken Steele's way was a lie. She did tolerate it more easily each time, and Steele always rewarded her for being a good girl. With his attentive care and the reassurance that the bad guy in the bank scandal and her assaulters were in jail, Ivy began to bristle slightly under Steele's control. Not enough to warrant a repeat of her buzzy lesson, but Ivy knew her brain was ready to get back to work.

When Steele laid her down on the bed in his welding area to take a nap, Ivy complained, "I can't take a nap all the time at work. I need to get ready to be productive all day long on Monday."

"We'll see how you feel on Monday. If it's too much, I'm sure the doctor will order shortened hours for a while," Steele said, tucking the covers around her neck and making sure her headphones were protecting her from the intensive noise filling the garage.

"I have to go back to work, Steele."

"Daddy."

She sighed dramatically and restated her response. "I have to go back to work, Daddy."

"I know. I'm going to make sure you're as ready to go as possible."

When he leaned in to kiss her forehead, Ivy felt her heart flutter. She loved him so much. Should she tell him?

Steele moved away to resume his work on the set of tailpipes on his workbench. He turned on the exhaust fan that whisked away any dangerous fumes and created a type of white noise that combined with her headphones, blocked everything out. He carefully protected her from the intense light of the welding flame. The molten metal that fused things together glowed red hot as he set the expertly welded parts aside to cool down.

She'd heard the other mechanics speaking of his talent in their conversations and discussions with owners looking to fix or upgrade some aspect of their ride. It was fascinating to watch him work, even from the distance he required her to stay.

Staying with the Shadowridge Guardians had opened her eyes to an entirely new world. Bikers had come into the bank with their leather attire, tattoos, and bad-boy ways, and Ivy hoped she'd treated them with the same courtesy and friendliness as she had anyone walking in wearing a suit. Now, after spending time in their world, Ivy could never treat them the same as everyone else.

These guys and their women and daughters had become her family. They'd protected her and welcomed her without a fuss or protest. She was Steele's, so she was theirs.

The motorcycle club members were completely different from the high-powered business people she was ashamed to admit she'd treated with deference. Those in suits would have walked away. Steele climbed into filth and sharp obstacles to save her. The other MC guys would have done the same without hesitating. She squeezed Lucky to her chest. They carried teddy bears, for goodness' sake.

A loud knock on the wall brought her head up. Kade stood a distance away from where Steele worked with an open flame.

The tough Enforcer waited patiently for the welder to finish his bead, turn off the torch, and remove the protective visor.

"There's a visitor for Ivy," he reported.

Kade's glower immediately ignited worry in Ivy's belly. She watched Steele process the information and nod. What was going on? She stood when Steele straightened and stripped off his heavy gloves.

"Well, Little girl. This is interesting. Let's go see what's happening."

Ivy nodded and trailed behind Steele's bulk, holding on to his cut to reassure herself. As they rounded the reception desk, she saw Mr. Harris, the bank president, holding a box of things. Ivy immediately recognized her photo frame sticking out of the top.

"Mr. Harris? What's going on?" she asked.

"I have transferred you to another branch. You'll work on Summerset Street starting on Monday," he reported, thrusting the box toward to her.

Steele quickly claimed the box from the bank president and set it to the side as Ivy searched for words. "There already is a bank manager at the Summerset branch. I am taking his place?"

"No, Edgar is remaining at Summerset," he said, before turning to leave.

Ivy let go of Steele's cut to dart forward, blocking his path. "There will be two bank managers at Summerset?"

"No. Edgar will remain the bank manager. You'll supervise the loan officers and report to him."

"You've demoted me because I discovered theft at the bank?" Her voice rose with indignation.

"Please stay in control, Miss Jenkins. I think I've seen enough theatrics with you. I demoted you because you no longer maintain a professional status in the community. Living in sin in the local motorcycle club hovel is not the profile the bank wishes to put into management positions. You, of course, can put in your notice, and I'm sure the remaining members of the board will allow you to have that applied retroactively to your sick time."

"Ahem," Steele cleared his throat ominously behind the bank president. After Mr. Harris turned to look at him from the corner of his eye, he rotated fully to face a line of Shadowridge Guardians, standing shoulder to shoulder behind him.

"Call off your thugs immediately, Miss Jenkins," he demanded with a tremor of nervousness shaking his words.

"These men aren't thugs, nor are they mine," Ivy pointed out before amending that statement. "Well, one is mine."

"Exactly. You've created quite the stir in the bank when you've visited with your… companion."

"Mr. Harris, I would urge you to reconsider targeting Ivy because of her association with the Shadowridge Guardians. I, for one, won't leave my money with a bank that discriminates against a talented bank officer due to who she chooses as friends," Steele said firmly.

"I'm sorry to hear that… Sir. I'm sure you'll find another bank more to your liking," Mr. Harris suggested.

"Who's in charge of the board now that Mr. Morton is in jail?" Ivy demanded.

"They have made me the interim board president as the board searches for a replacement," Mr. Harris said, puffing out his chest with obvious self-importance.

"I will contact the board's secretary on Monday to schedule a meeting," Ivy said firmly.

"I'm afraid it will be a very long time before we deal with inconsequential matters. The board will focus on rebuilding," Mr. Harris said, sealing her fate. "Would you like to give me your verbal notice?"

"No, thank you, Mr. Harris," Ivy answered, barely keeping it under control at the audacity of the bank officer.

"You may rethink that decision at any time this weekend. Just leave a message on my voicemail at the bank," he encouraged as he turned to walk out of the motorcycle repair shop.

Steele stepped forward, and the weasel took a step away, bumping into a workbench and wiping grease onto his immaculate suit jacket. Mr. Harris focused on that with a tsk of disapproval. He pulled a white handkerchief from his pocket to dab at the stain, spreading it and turning a corner of the pristine cloth gray.

Muttering about the blotch and the cleaning bill, Mr. Harris walked out of the repair shop without a look behind him.

"You want me to make sure his fancy car doesn't run on Monday morning?" Talon sneered.

"While that pleases me to imagine his reaction, I think there's a better way to handle Mr. Harris," Steele responded, chopping off any retribution plans.

"Really? What are we going to do?" Ivy asked.

"It's better that you don't know," Steele told her.

"Don't do anything to get yourself in trouble, Steele. That won't help my case that I'm not hanging with the wrong kind of people," Ivy warned quickly.

"I'll take care of him."

Ivy talked to him until she was hoarse. Steele wouldn't explain what he had in mind, and the others professed their lack of knowledge.

By dinnertime, she'd decided that maybe her arguments had finally sunk into Steele's brain and he'd reconsidered. The group hung out together in the common room as normal. No one mentioned Mr. Harris, the bank, or Ivy's job. She relaxed a bit and enjoyed the tough banter she'd learned covered a deep commitment to each other.

Ivy loved being here with Steele. She could sit on his lap and no one commented. He could pull her close for a kiss or send her over to get a napkin and swat her bottom sharply. No one even seemed to notice—or if they did, their response was an indulgent smile or a grouchy comment about needing to find their own Little.

Since it was Friday night, Steele allowed Ivy to stay up past her bedtime. Finally, her yawns won out, and she cuddled against his chest. Looping her hands around his neck, she clung to Steele as he carried her back to his apartment as everyone wished her a good night. She waved lazily and stayed in that foggy, almost asleep state as Steele undressed her and tucked her into bed. Ivy listened to Steele move around the room quietly until she couldn't keep her sweet dreams away.

CHAPTER
EIGHTEEN

"Daddy?" Ivy reached a hand out to search for Steele's warmth. He always slept wrapped around her when she woke up in the dark. His side of the bed was cold.

Ivy pushed herself up on one elbow to look around. The bedroom was completely silent, and she didn't hear anything from the adjoining sitting room. Heeding her need to use the restroom, she crept into the bathroom, thankful for the nightlight he always turned on for her.

Still no response from the protective man as she emerged from the bathroom. Opening the cracked door separating the bedroom and the family room, Ivy called, "Daddy?" The room was completely empty.

"Where'd you go?" she asked aloud and then felt silly for talking to no one.

She couldn't go out in the main area dressed in an oversized T-shirt and no panties. Quickly, Ivy turned on a light and pulled some clothes out of one drawer where Steele had stowed some of her clothes. She'd protested that she didn't need three of the four drawers in his dresser, but he'd just laughed.

"Little girls have lots of pretty clothes. Your Daddy doesn't."

It made sense when she looked at it that way. Steele wore the same thing every day. Battered jeans with spark marks burned into the fabric, T-shirts that fit snug across his muscular chest, and leather boots completed his look before he donned the heavy leather welding apron. Ivy did need a variety of things to wear.

She peeked out the door, listening for the men's voices. Maybe they were having some sort of meeting or playing pool. When she heard nothing, she crept toward the gathering room. Ivy finally heard a whisper of sound at the end of the hallway. Peering around the corner, she felt the corners of her lips quirk upward when she saw a round bottom sticking out of the refrigerator. The all-black clothing clued her in immediately to who it was.

"Remi?"

The young woman whirled around, clutching a can of spray whipped cream to her chest. "Oh! Ivy! You scared me!"

"Got something planned?" Ivy asked, feeling herself grin widely as her eyebrows waggled suggestively almost by themselves. Standing in the bright lighting, Remi looked starkly Goth. A thought popped into Ivy's head at Remi's Goth look. *I wonder what she'd look like with a clean-scrubbed face wearing something—pink?*

"What?" Remi looked down at the item in her hand and laughed. "You're bad. I got hungry hanging around and decided to make a snack. Want a hot fudge sundae with me?"

Ivy hadn't been hungry until she heard those magical words together: fudge and sundae. "I'd love one. Extra whipped cream on mine."

Remi gathered the other ingredients for the treat while Ivy ran to grab bowls and spoons. Chatting happily, Ivy took care of microwaving the glass jar of hot fudge as Remi scooped up a generous ball of vanilla ice cream into each dish.

"I noticed cinnamon ice cream in the freezer, too. Want to

experiment with cinnamon and chocolate?" Remi asked, clicking the ice cream scoop on the countertop.

"I bet it's wonderful," Ivy agreed with a nod.

"Me, too!"

In a few minutes, they'd crafted gorgeous sundaes. Remi handed the can of whipped cream to Ivy. "This stuff is so good."

"Even if it's not used for sexy times?" Ivy teased and laughed at her own silliness in thinking Remi was romantically involved with one of the Shadowridge Guardians instead of just visiting there frequently to see her father.

"You're bad," Remi accused with a laugh. "I'm glad you're here, Ivy. You fit well with the group."

The two took big bites of their sundaes and groaned with delight. It was so good. Eating the delicious treat consumed their attention for several bites.

Finally, Ivy asked, "Where is everyone? I woke up and Steele was gone."

"And he didn't tell you where they went?"

"No. He was just gone. Do you know what's up?"

Remi took a big bite of ice cream. Ivy suspected it was to keep from answering her question, and then Remi smiled as the sound of motorcycle engines rumbled through the exterior doors. "They're back. Steele can answer your question."

"Uh-oh. That's not good," Ivy said, feeling doom lurking. She took another bite of her sundae to distract herself.

The men walked in loud and boisterous.

"Did you see that guy's face? I think he almost peed his pants," Talon joked.

"I think he did," Storm confirmed.

"I don't think she'll have any more..." Rock's voice faded away as they saw the women at the counter. "Hi, ladies."

"We're having fudge sundaes, Dad," Remi explained.

"While the cat's away, the mice will play?" Kade asked. His growly, deep voice made both Littles shiver. "Cold?"

"Ice cream," Remi sassed.

"Hmmm."

Steele was the last one through the door. The men parted for him to walk toward Ivy. "Hi, Emerald Eyes. Couldn't sleep?"

"I woke up and everyone was gone," Ivy said before shrugging and waving her spoon toward Remi. "Well, almost everyone. Remi suggested sundaes. Where have you all been?"

"Mmm, let me have a bite." Steele plucked the spoon from her hand and scooped up an enormous portion.

The muffled sound of appreciation that came from Steele's mouth made Ivy blush. It was almost the same noise he made when eating her. Squeezing her legs together, she struggled not to be distracted.

"It is good, isn't it? So… What were you doing?"

"Official Guardian business, Ivy," Steele answered as he scooped her bowl off the counter and took her hand to tug her off the stool.

He looked past Ivy at Remi and said, "Thanks. I owe you one."

Everything clicked into place for Ivy, and she met Remi's gaze. "You were babysitting me?"

"Just hanging out, Ivy," Remi rushed to reassure her before saying to Steele, "Taking care of family."

He nodded his agreement with that meaningful statement. "Come on, Ivy. Let's take this treat back to our apartment," Steele suggested, pulling gently on her hand.

Ivy didn't resist. She had some questions for her Daddy. Some tough questions. Pacing down the hall, she tried to choose what she should ask first. Once in the apartment, Steele led her to the couch and sat down next to her.

"This is really great, Little girl." He scooped a spoonful of the delicious mixture out of the bowl and held it to her lips.

Clamping her lips closed, she shook her head. One part of her mind was pleased to find she hadn't gotten discombobulated by the motion. She must be healing.

Thrusting that out of her thoughts, Ivy asked, "What were you all doing?"

Steele shrugged and ate the bite of the ice cream mixture. She sat there impatiently, waiting for him to finish. "I'm not going to forget what I asked you if you keep your mouth full," she warned.

"Don't take that tone with me, Little girl," Steele said with raised eyebrows.

"Can you just tell me why everyone was gone? And who peed their pants?"

"No one peed—at least in their pants," Steele assured her and held a bite to her lips.

Annoyed, Ivy ate it. The bowl would have to be empty soon. *Ooh! The cinnamon is good with chocolate syrup!*

Now peeved at herself, Ivy swallowed hard and choked.

"Careful, Little girl," Steele warned, patting her gently on her back.

"Will you just tell me?" she asked as soon as she could breathe.

"There are some things that I'll never tell you, Little girl. Things that are only Shadowridge Guardians' business. You'll have to accept that, Ivy." His unyielding gaze held hers.

"But I think it was about me," she countered.

"That doesn't make any difference. This was Shadowridge Guardians' business."

Ivy reached out to grab hold of the edge of Steele's cut as she studied his face. She'd done that so many times since he'd rescued her. The worn leather felt so familiar to her touch. It reassured her more than anything. It was definitely more encouraging than his stern look.

"Steele, I'm a grown woman." She waved a hand around the room. "I mean, I love being Little here—being your Little. But out here, I have to be a professional and in charge. Did you all do anything because Mr. Harris demoted me?"

"We didn't do anything, Little girl. We just provided transportation for someone with their head screwed on right. I'm glad to know others see exactly what Mr. Harris is."

"What he is?" Ivy echoed in concern. "Come on, Steele. You've got to tell me what's going on."

"Report to your bank on Monday," he told her before taking another bite of her ice cream.

"My regular bank branch? Not Summerset?"

"Your bank, like normal. Here, help me eat this. You don't want me to get a pot belly," he suggested, holding another bite to her lips.

Accepting the treat, Ivy climbed onto his lap and leaned against Steele's broad chest. "You saved me again, didn't you?"

"You save me every day, Little girl. You have more power than you realize," he said, kissing her gently. "Mmm, cinnamon and chocolate may be my favorite flavor. I wonder if there's any more whipped cream left in that can?"

"You can't go get it," she hissed. "They'll all know."

"They already know, Ivy," he said, running his finger around the inside of the bowl to scoop up some deliciousness and place it in her mouth. He growled at the feel of her mouth sucking lightly on his finger.

"You are going to be the end of me."

Steele supported her as he leaned forward to set the bowl on the coffee table before reaching over his shoulder to tug his T-shirt off in a display of muscles that instantly turned her on. There was no pot belly there. She traced a line down the center of his abdomen and felt him chuckle as he obviously read her thought. He spread the cotton fabric over the empty section of the couch.

"Come here, Little girl." Steele wrapped his arms around her to hold her steady as he turned to stretch out on the couch.

Propped up on her arms, she looked at him with wide eyes as she tried to understand what he was doing. Ivy watched Steele reach for the leg of the coffee table and pull it closer to the couch.

He dipped his finger once again into the melting mixture and drew a line down the side of his throat.

"Taste me, Ivy."

She leaned forward to lick the liquid from his skin before it could roll too far down his throat and soak into the couch. Ivy hadn't thought the sundae could taste any better. She was totally wrong. Lapping her tongue over his warm skin, she savored the combination of Steele's unique flavor and heat.

Ivy could feel his response to her diligence in licking all the stickiness from his skin. She wiggled on top of his body as he hardened under her. His shaft pressed against her mound, demanding attention.

Whack! She lifted her head to look down at him at the sting of his swat.

"What?"

"Lift your bottom, Little girl," he growled.

Afraid she'd done something wrong, Ivy hesitated. *Whack!* She raised her pelvis from his in a hurry.

"Good girl."

His hand swept under her body to unfasten his pants. She tried not to rub herself on his fingers as he brushed her mound. Ivy bit her bottom lip, trying desperately not to reveal how aroused she was. Her breath caught in her throat when he cupped her heat.

"It's okay, Ivy. Together, we're combustible. That's how it's supposed to be. If you don't react to the feel of your Daddy's body or touch, that's when I worry—not when you need me more than your next breath."

She nodded, not really knowing what she agreed with, but loving his words. Steele always seemed to be a step ahead of her. He just got her.

"Make love to me?" she asked.

"Eventually, Little girl. Right now, you need some playtime."

He shifted one hand from her mound to bracket her waist with both. Sweeping under her leggings, Steele drew the stretchy fabric over her hips and down her thighs, leaving her clad only in her skimpy panties. Those he traced underneath the lacy edge along the sensitive curve of her bottom. She shivered and tried to remain above him, but his touch made it tougher every second.

"On me, sweetheart. I need to feel you against me."

Without a second's hesitation, she lowered herself to him and froze. She could feel his thick cock pressing against her body. The thin silk fabric of her underwear was the only thing separating her from his heated shaft.

A moan slipped from her lips as he cupped her bottom with open hands and rubbed her against him. "Please, Steele."

"We're not rushing this, Little girl. I haven't had my dessert yet," he answered as he continued to stroke her over his body.

"Dessert?" she echoed, unable to concentrate on anything else as captivating tingles gathered between her legs. Surely he couldn't make her come just from rubbing against her panties.

Steele curled up from the couch to nibble at the cord of her throat. The searing heat of his mouth seemed to zing through her body. Ivy knew the delight his lips and tongue could lavish on her pussy. The memory of his skill dwelt in her brain as he continued to move her over him, speeding up the motion to intensify her pleasure.

Suddenly, it was all too much. Ivy combusted into a climax that seemed to shake her whole body. The pressure of her pussy against his rigid shaft was too much and not enough at the same time. She panted with need.

"I've got you, Ivy. I'll make it even better." Steele shifted her legs to the side as he sat up fully with her cradled against his torso. Capturing her lips, he kissed her deeply.

Ivy clung to his broad shoulders as she kissed him back with all the emotions swirling inside her. His hands stroked down her sides to grip the bottom of Ivy's shirt. Ripping his mouth from hers, Steele stripped the T-shirt from her body, leaving her clad only in those drenched panties as he tossed it away.

"Damn, Little girl. You're so beautiful." Hooking his fingers into the sides of her last remaining garment, he tore the miniscule scrap of fabric away.

With a gasp, she sat up taller, presenting herself to his view as he reached blindly for that bowl. Ivy watched as his hand returned with a fingertip dipped in the melting creaminess. Her heart fluttered in her chest as he drew a line from her collarbone to her nipple, leaving a wet trail to the budded target. She held her breath as he leaned forward to taste the sweetness on her skin. When he took too long to kiss the path away, Ivy cupped her breasts and offered them to him.

"Please?"

"I'm going to get there, Emerald Eyes. I'm in charge."

"But…"

"No buts, Little girl. Daddy's in charge."

She heard herself whimper as he continued his slow pace to his final destination. When his mouth closed over her taut peak, she gasped in reaction as his tongue swirled around her, teasing and tantalizing.

One of his hands drew a line down her stomach to the top of her mound, making her dig her fingertips into the muscles of his shoulders. Willing him to touch her more intimately, Ivy tried to hold still, but she vibrated with desire. That first orgasm had only pushed her need for Steele higher. He traced down her cleft, sliding through the slick juices gathered there. She barely breathed as he stroked through her pink folds to tap lightly on her clit.

This time, her moan interrupted his caresses. She protested when he lifted her to stand on her feet. "Don't stop!"

"Go get me a condom, sweetheart."

She turned on a dime and ran for the nightstand where he kept the protection. Fumbling the drawer open, Ivy grabbed a packet and pulled out three. Not waiting to separate one from the strip, Ivy turned to run back to Steele only to skid to a halt at the sight of his muscular bare butt, pointing her way as he leaned over to pull his socks off.

He stood and turned around to find her braced against the door frame with the trio of packets in her hand. "Got big plans?" he teased.

Instead of being embarrassed, Ivy felt so comfortable with him that she twirled the strip in a circle. "I might."

"Let's start with one, Little girl," he suggested, stalking forward to wrap his arms around her waist to lift her feet off the floor before returning to the couch to take a seat.

When he reached for the condoms, she held them away. Answering the silent question his arched eyebrow asked, Ivy said, "Daddy, can I have some more ice cream? I only got to taste you once."

His hands tightened on her waist before he dropped the packets to the seat next to him and nodded. "Play, Ivy."

She slid over his thighs, pushing the coffee table to make room, and settled on her knees between his legs. Mirroring his devastating touch, Ivy trailed her fingers from his knees along his inner thighs. When his eyes became hooded, she knew she had his full attention. Ivy leaned forward to blow a thin trail of warm breath from the root of his thick erection to the broad tip, watching it jerk in reaction. Unable to resist, she leaned in and kissed the head.

Steele threaded his fingers through her hair and pulled her closer with a groan.

"Silly me. I forgot the ice cream," she whispered against his skin.

"You are going to kill me," he claimed as he loosened his hold long enough for her to turn the opposite way and scoop up a bit of the melted ice cream.

She could feel him watching her like a hawk as she turned back to him. Ivy reached out her right hand to wrap around his shaft and pull it toward her. It pulsed in her palm and she rotated her grip to leave the top bare and drew a quick inhale of breath from Steele, which turned to a low hiss as she drew a line of melted ice cream up his cock to the broad head.

She leaned forward to lick away the small lines of cream before they dropped to the floor. Steele tightened his fingers that cupped her head. Tangling his grip in her hair, he drew her mouth to the end of his erection and growled, "Open your mouth, Ivy."

She leaned forward, loving the prickle of not quite pain as he held her securely. After pressing a light kiss to his cock, she opened her mouth around him and swooped forward to engulf as much of his thick erection as she could. Taking a shaky breath, Ivy backed away slightly.

"Relax your throat," he sternly demanded.

Being under his control thrilled her. Eager to please him, she followed his directions. This time, she took more of his length, loving the sounds he made and the pulsing strength of the shaft inside her. As his praise wrapped around her, Ivy felt powerful and loved that she pleased him.

A small ripping sound made Ivy panic as the memory of duct tape being torn from the roll rebounded into her mind. With all her strength, she pushed back violently from Steele. Shoving the coffee table out of the way, she backed to the wall and huddled, wary. Her breath came fast and harsh as her instincts took over and Ivy assessed the room for danger.

She felt awful when she realized what she had done. It was just the two of them. Steele wouldn't hurt her. He'd saved her.

He rose naked from the couch and stalked forward. She braced herself for reassurances and comfort. That wasn't what she wanted or needed. He dropped to his knees before her and settled his hands on either side of her body. The fierce look on his face didn't scare her, but gave her strength.

"Fight, Ivy. Never give in."

She bolted to her knees and slammed her lips against his, dominating the kiss and taking control. Steele challenged her, not making it easy on her but asking for everything. Ivy pulled back and glared at him.

Steele met that look without flinching. "Whatever you need, Little girl. I'm here."

She launched herself forward, pushing him back onto the floor. Ivy straddled his body, hovering over him. He gripped her thighs, aiding her balance as he waited to see what she would do next. When he didn't move, she dropped to her hands and knees over him and leaned forward to bite his shoulder. His hands tightened around her before one released her and swatted her bottom sharply.

The sting drew her head up as desire flooded back into her body like a tidal wave. "I need you inside me."

His hand searched the floor by his side. "Here." He handed her a bright pink condom, and she realized when he'd opened it that had been the sound she'd heard.

"You put it on," he demanded.

She rose to her knees and, with his help, fitted the rubber over his erection. His flesh throbbed in her grasp and her sense of power swelled as she settled over him, placing the broad head to her opening. Slowly, she sank down, feeling him stretch and challenge her to take him inside. His dark eyes held her captive. When her pelvis reached his, those deep brown eyes said everything.

He was proud of her.

"I love you, Little girl."

"I love you, too, Daddy. I'm sorry."

"Never apologize, Ivy," he corrected her gruffly. "We all have our demons. We'll deal with ours together."

When she nodded, he continued in a low, tortured groan, "Now move before you kill me, Emerald Eyes."

Their lovemaking was fierce and demanding. She was in control, but Steele drew everything from her as they crashed together. Their bodies heated the room, bringing a sheen to their skin. Pleasure built inside them, driving their motion.

"Ahhh!" Ivy screamed into the room, and Steele drove upward quickly three times before joining her climax.

He gathered her limp body against him, holding her tight as she processed through her emotions. She felt balanced for the first time since the attack. Ivy could never fight off three large men. She'd tried her best and had never given up. Listening to Steele's thudding heartbeat, she knew he had saved her not only physically, but mentally. He was there for her.

CHAPTER
NINETEEN

Ivy parked her car in the back of the bank parking lot on Monday and took a big breath and released it. She was excited to get back to work but anxious about dealing with Mr. Harris. Finally, she grabbed her purse and forced herself to open the door and slide out.

Automatically, she headed for the back door and slowed as she reached the beginning of the shadows that gathered there. Maybe she should walk in the front for a while. Her key wouldn't work there until the lobby opened. She'd have to knock on the window to have someone let her inside.

"Ivy! Hi! Let me walk in with you. We're so glad you're back," Virginia said warmly.

"Hi. Thanks."

As they approached, a huge floodlight clicked on, illuminating the area. It totally erased the trace of darkness from the entrance. Ivy felt her heart rate slow. This was so much better.

"Wait until you see the display inside. No more relying only on the peephole," Virginia celebrated.

As she stepped inside, Ivy turned to see a video feed of the back of the building. Not just the area around the door, but the display revealed the entire back of the building.

"Mr. Harris did this?" Ivy asked.

"Oh, no! Some generous donor insisted on updating the technology. He paid for all the costs from the installer the board approved," Virginia told her as they walked through the employee area to reach the lobby.

Claps filled the area as people spotted her. Busy with all the morning duties required to open the bank on time, they waved and called their warm greetings to welcome her back as Ivy passed. Stepping into her office, she found the box of her belongings set in the middle of her desk as well as a gorgeous bouquet.

Ivy collapsed into her chair and opened the bottom drawer of her desk to stow her purse. There, a small version of Lucky dressed in a tattered vest peered up at her. Blinking away the tears, she caressed his soft head. She wasn't alone.

To distract herself, Ivy plucked the card from the flowers. It was from one of the bank board members, Erick Hamilton. He'd risen through the ranks quickly and quietly to claim a seat. She stared at it. What could make him send her flowers? Maybe he was the friend of the doctors?

Forcing her mind back to getting ready, Ivy quickly unpacked her box of possessions. Setting her nameplate on her desk, she felt official. She grabbed her mug and headed for the coffeepot, greeting people as she passed. The last office in the row was dark. Mr. Harris wasn't always in the bank during all the official business hours, of course, but Ivy was amazed that he hadn't been here to make sure she'd followed his instructions.

She filled her cup only partially and felt guilty. Steele hadn't let her drink caffeine at all while she'd recuperated. Even though he wasn't here to see her, she only put a splash in her cup with some milk and sugar.

Taking a sip, she smiled. *Perfect!*

Checking in with all the departments as she had always done before the bank opened, Ivy was pleased to find everyone glad to have her back. When they tried to tell her horror stories of what happened while she was gone, Ivy had waved them off and asked them to submit a report through the normal channels if there was something injurious to the bank customers or themselves, the security at the bank, or against board policy. She didn't want a lot of hearsay. To take something to the board, she would need concrete evidence. To her amazement, many confessed that they already had filed complaints.

Ivy hung in the lobby, talking to customers entering for the first hour until the morning rush subsided. It felt good that the regulars had missed her. Some had even heard of the attack and expressed indignation and concern that there wasn't better security. She did her best to address their worries and shared that improvements had been made to keep everyone safe and to protect the bank even more.

By the time she wandered back to her office, Ivy was glad to have some time alone. She had interacted with more people than she'd talked to in two weeks. Checking her schedule, Ivy noted she didn't have any requests for meetings. *Probably because Mr. Harris booted me out of here.*

Instead of diving into a sea of ill will toward her boss, Ivy continued working on her computer and checked her messages. The number that had accumulated astounded her. Two weeks' worth of bank business stared at her from the inbox. Taking a fortified drink of her coffee-flavored milk, Ivy dived in.

An hour later, a knock on her door made her look up with a smile, expecting to see an employee needing assistance. To her surprise, three board members stood at her door. *What is going on now?*

"Gentlemen," she greeted them as she stood. "I don't think you're here simply to welcome me back."

"Welcome back," one said warmly, and her level of concern lowered—a bit.

"Shall we go into the conference room?" Ivy suggested.

A few minutes later, they settled around a large table with coffee. Ivy took a sip herself to calm her nerves before asking, "Who would like to update me?"

"I'm here as the newly elected board president," Erick Hamilton began. "Unfortunate circumstances have forced a lot of changes in a very short time. On behalf of the board, I would like to apologize for the circumstances that we believe caused you being targeted—twice."

"Something other than Mr. Morton's removal from the board?" she asked, leaning forward. "Shouldn't Mr. Harris be here? He told me he was the interim president."

"Mr. Harris is no longer a bank employee and never was a board member," Erick Hamilton explained.

"I see."

"Friday night, a group of motorcycle riders came to visit me. I believe you know them—The Shadowridge Guardians?" When she nodded, trying to contain her astonishment, he continued, "After asking if I was the board member who golfed with your doctor at the hospital, a man named Steele requested I join them on a ride."

Ivy crossed her fingers under the table. What had they done? Her brain followed that thought immediately with, How did Steele know that Mr. Morton wasn't the friend of the doctor? Immediately, she realized she should have figured that out. Mr. Morton wasn't anyone's friend. He must have heard Erick speaking about the doctor's recommendations.

"You told Mr. Morton I'd be out for an extra week?" she guessed.

"I did. It was the least we could do."

"And you went on a ride with the Guardians?"

"I'm not normally a motorcycle club member, but Steele stated they were on their way to see Mr. Harris and thought I would be interested in the conversation. Since Mr. Harris's name appeared in reports several times while you were gone and he appeared to be trying to seize control of the board, I thought it was worth the gamble."

"You rode with the Guardians?" she repeated. "On a motorcycle?"

"I did. It was quite invigorating. I may have to buy myself a bike now."

He waved away that thought and continued. "Arriving at Mr. Harris's house, the group parked legally on the street in front of his house and waited. I stayed in the background—in the shadows—so he wouldn't recognize me. A few minutes later, he peeked out the door to tell everyone that he had called the police and that they were on the way."

Mr. Hamilton looked at the other men and chuckled. "I would have called one of you for bail money. My wife would have left me there."

The laughter broke the tension slightly, and Ivy had to smile.

"Steele addressed him politely and pointed out that they were gathered on the public street, which was perfectly legal. They would be glad to wait until Mr. Harris had time to talk to them. Mr. Harris decided to do that thirty minutes later when the police still hadn't arrived and the neighbors were beginning to gather. It turns out the Guardians support Shadowridge in a variety of ways."

"They certainly have helped me," Ivy pointed out.

"And many other people as well. When Mr. Harris emerged, Steele spoke to him so everyone could hear. During their conversation, Mr. Harris revealed he lacked the professional and social skills needed in a man we choose to have as a bank president. I took the opportunity to videotape the encounter and showed that to my colleagues early this morning. They convened a board meeting and made the tough decisions we needed."

"What did he do?" Ivy asked in shock.

"Quite literally, he behaved like a jerk and relied on victim shaming to explain his lack of action and leadership. Frothing at the mouth and waving a gun at the public does not encourage people to trust our bank and invest their hard-earned money here. His demeanor changed tremendously when I walked forward for him to recognize me while I continued to record."

Ivy stared at him in shock. Her stomach sank. "Victim shaming?"

"Yes. On behalf of the board and of me personally, we would like to apologize for the unprofessionalism you've dealt with while employed under his tenure here. A letter of commendation is now in your file. Here is a copy for your records," he said, sliding a file folder across the table to her. "Your annual review will be completed this week and you will find that your efforts to protect the bank's interests by exposing Mr. Morton and Mr. Harris have been rewarded. We would ask one more thing of you."

Completely mind-boggled, she asked, "Yes?"

"One of the board's requirements for a bank president is that they have a master's degree in finance or a related area. We would like to add reimbursement of successful graduate courses completed to your contract and to encourage you to pursue an advanced degree," Mr. Hamilton suggested.

"Are you suggesting I could be the next bank president?" she clarified.

"No one has a crystal ball to see the future, but you have a brilliant career ahead of you. You were the only one to note a problem in the first place and document it. Then you continued to follow the data trail to discover the theft went deeper than believed. We would like to support your career and hope that you'll consider applying for that position when you finish your degree."

"I will. Thank you. And I will take advantage of the chance to expand my knowledge with a degree program. That is very generous," Ivy said in amazement.

The three men stood and shook her hand. She followed them to the door and thanked them again.

Mr. Hamilton drew her aside to hand her his card. "Here is my personal phone number. Do not hesitate to call."

"Thank you for the flowers."

"My pleasure. The Shadowridge Guardians also gave me a

bear last night. I hope you found it. I wanted you to know that you had a friend here when you walked in today."

Holding the folder to her chest, Ivy nodded. She was completely out of words as the kind man turned and walked out the door. On autopilot, she walked to her office and closed the door. No one would disturb her unless it was an emergency.

Parking her car next to the Shadowridge compound that evening, Ivy walked to the garage area and noted most people had finished for the day. The others greeted her fondly as she passed. Steele was exactly where she expected him to be—at his bench, hard at work.

She took a seat on the cot behind him and waited patiently for him to notice her or finish. It didn't take long. Steele extinguished the torch and stood, shrugging off the protective helmet. He brushed a hand over his protective leather apron to make sure no molten sparks smoldered before stalking forward to extend a hand to help her to her feet. Wrapping his arms around her, Steele hugged her tight.

When Ivy felt the light kiss on her temple, she relaxed into her Daddy's arms. "I expected you there when I walked out tonight."

"I chained myself here."

Ivy understood. He would have fought himself not to walk her out of that back entrance for the first time. She leaned back slightly to look into his eyes. "You were right. I needed to do it myself. I did, of course, follow protocol and walk out with several other employees after checking the additional security that's been added."

"I knew you could do it," he praised and kissed her lightly.

"I had a visit from Erick Hamilton today," she shared.

Steele's gaze never wavered. "I like him."

"I do, too. You know that could have backfired horribly."

"That wasn't a possibility," Steele rebutted her statement. His tone once again brooked no argument.

"What did Mr. Harris do?"

"You don't want to know."

"Okay. They want me to go to school, so I will qualify to be a bank president," Ivy told him.

"No late nights, Little girl. You need your sleep." Before she could protest, he added, "I'll support you in every way, but I'm always going to take care of you."

There was no argument to that. She knew Steele would always be there for her, but he'd always be in charge.

"I don't want to go back to my house. Can I stay here with you?" she asked.

A devastating smile spread across his lips, and she shivered against him in reaction to his potent charm. His arms tightened around her, hugging her closer. "I'm glad that was your idea. Your place is always with me, Little girl."

"The guys won't mind?"

"All old ladies are welcome here."

"Do I have to be an old lady?" she asked, bristling at that name.

"Nope. You get to be my Little girl."

"Do the others know?"

"Yes. I'm not the only Daddy in the Guardians."

"Kade?"

Steele's slow nod confirmed her suspicion.

"Mr. Hamilton wants to buy a bike now."

"That doesn't surprise me."

"Are you ever going to take me on a ride?" she asked.

"As soon as we get clearance from the doctor. I don't want your brain vibrated until we're sure you're okay. How did it go using the computer today?"

"I have a headache," Ivy confessed and felt one of his hands stroke up her back to massage her neck gently.

"Your muscles are as rigid as a board. Dinner and a hot bath for you before bed," he announced.

"Sounds heavenly, Daddy."

CHAPTER
TWENTY

By the end of the week, the excitement of being back at work had evaporated. Mr. Harris wasn't there to give her more work and correct all her efforts, but he also wasn't there to do his own work. Another bank manager had come to help, but there was definitely a learning curve to understanding everything that needed to be done and what the previous bank president had completed.

Friday afternoon, a large rumble drew Ivy from her office. It sounded a few blocks away—even through the thick walls of the bank. The throb of the thunderous motors grew as something approached. Virginia joined her at the large plate-glass windows as others craned their necks to see.

"I have a guess," Virginia whispered.

"Surely not."

"Want to bet? Go get your purse," the loyal employee encouraged.

"That doesn't set an outstanding example for everyone else working until closing," Ivy stated with a shake of her head. "If it's them, they'll wait for me to finish."

"I'm sure they will." Virginia hurried away to start a fire

under the employees. They had one more reason to get out of there efficiently on a Friday.

When the bikes came into view, Ivy stepped outside to watch them. She grinned at the tough-looking motorcycle club. Ivy definitely wouldn't recommend tangling with them—the Shadowridge Guardians lurked on the edges of societal rules. She knew, however, that they'd do anything to help her and others who needed them. Plus, knowing they all had teddy bears in their saddlebags lessened their rough appearances.

She waved as they drove into the parking lot. Faust, Rock, Storm, Doc, Bear, Talon, Silver, and Gabriel led the group with others she didn't know as well, following. Steele and Storm rounded out the group. The men backed into parking spaces toward the back of the parking lot so they didn't interfere with the bank patrons. Ivy skipped across the pavement to greet them.

"Hi! Wow! You guys are impressive together," she complimented them.

"That's exactly the impression we want to give the world." Talon's usual sarcasm made her smile.

"Hey, Little girl. You ready to go for a ride?" Steele strolled forward.

Ivy looked around, embarrassed to see if any bank patrons overheard his words. She should have known Steele would have already made sure everything was safe.

"I need to stay. It will be about thirty minutes. Is that okay?"

"Of course it is. We'll hang in the parking lot and make friends," Storm replied.

"Try to smile every once in a while, will you? Don't scare everyone," she suggested.

"We'll be on our best behavior," Rock assured her.

Ivy looked at him, assessing whether she could trust the elder biker and decided quickly that he was sincere. Besides, he was Remi's dad, and she liked Remi a lot. Shaking her head, she walked forward to Steele and rose on her toes to wrap her arms around his neck.

"I won't be long," she assured before planting a quick kiss on his lips.

"A promise and a tease of a kiss. I guess you are feeling better." Steele looked over her head at Doc and gave him a thumbs up.

"Daddy!" she hissed. Everyone didn't need to know that Doc had given her a checkup last night.

"It's okay, sweetheart. They're all tickled you're feeling better. Go finish your day and then we'll go celebrate," Steele suggested.

"I'll be fast."

Dropping one last kiss on his lips, Ivy turned and walked as quickly as she could on her pumps. She wondered if being in a relationship with Steele would keep her from advancing at the bank. With a shrug of her shoulders, Ivy dismissed that idea. What was more important? Treasuring the special connection she had with the man who saved her and captured her heart or letting others decide how she lived her life? Ivy would choose Steele every day.

For once, closing the bank for the day was hassle-free. All the tellers balanced their drawers quickly and headed out with big smiles. Virginia helped Ivy finalize the rest of the accounts, and they were ready to leave in no time. Ivy looked at the woman who had become a good friend. When higher positions opened, Virginia would be the first candidate that would come to her mind.

"Come on, boss. They're waiting for you."

"It's best not to keep them standing around," Ivy agreed, grabbing her purse from her desk.

Even with the Shadowridge Guardians in the parking lot, Ivy took time to check all the security cameras. She definitely didn't want history to repeat itself. None of the Guardians appeared in the displays. They were standing far from the exit of the building. Ivy knew they had the area perfectly under control, even if she couldn't see them.

After exiting the building, Ivy pushed the door closed and waited to hear the security lock engage. With a goodnight to Virginia, Ivy headed for the man who waited for her.

"Should I follow you somewhere?" she asked, waving at her car.

"You'll ride with me," Steele stated firmly, holding up an extra helmet.

"But my car…"

"Your car was safe here for over a week. It will be okay overnight. You'll ride with me."

"O-Okay." She allowed him to fit the helmet onto her head and buckle it securely.

"Does that feel okay? Not too tight?"

"No. It's fine."

"Flip the visor down when we get started. That will keep the wind and bugs out of your eyes."

"Maybe…" She looked back at her car.

"You're going to love this, Little girl. Trust me."

That's all it took. If Steele asked her to trust him, she was there. The massive man had never lied to her. Straightening her shoulders, she nodded.

"Good girl." He stroked his hands over her shoulders before shrugging out of his leather jacket and helping her into the enormous garment. "When I lean, you lean. When we stop, you sit still. Got it?"

This time when she nodded, Steele patted her bottom before taking her purse. "Get on after me."

He stowed her handbag in a saddlebag. She peeked but couldn't see a stuffie hiding inside. With that taken care of, Steele swung a leg over the bike and started it with a powerful kick before knocking the stand back. Bracing the bike, he told her, "When you're ready."

She tried to be graceful as she followed his example, but Ivy felt completely uncoordinated. Thank goodness she'd chosen to wear pants that day. The oversized jacket was heavy and cumbersome by itself. If she'd tried to maneuver her way onto the seat in a skirt, she would have given someone a show. When she finally settled in place, Steele sat down as well. He pointed out the pegs for her feet and frowned at her pumps.

"I should have brought you some boots. I'll ride carefully, Emerald Eyes. I don't want to scuff those designer shoes."

"They're not important, Steele. I've got three other pairs of black dress shoes at home."

"Boots next time. Watch out for the pipes. They're hot and will burn you." She leaned to the side to see where he pointed and nodded.

"Is there more?" Ivy asked nervously.

"Now, it's time for fun. Relax and enjoy the feeling of freedom. It's time to fly."

Steele patted her hand reassuringly and drew it from resting on her thigh to wrap her arm around his waist. Repeating the action on the other side, he tugged her forward, and she slid on the leather seat to rest against his back—and his backside. "Hold tight. Yell in my ear if you need to stop for any reason."

"I'm ready." Ivy was proud there was only a small quiver in her voice.

The other men had mounted up when Steele started his bike. Storm and Bear eased into motion, and the others fell in behind them. Steele and Ivy were in the middle of the pack, with Doc next to her. She had a feeling the medic wanted to keep an eye on her.

The first few turns were scary, but Steele taught Ivy what to do by trapping her against his hard body. Soon she was so focused on the feel of the hot man in front of her that Ivy didn't worry as they navigated through several streets. She tensed a little as they got on the interstate, but the group stayed together wrapped around her.

The buzz between her legs grew stronger at the faster rate.

She clung to Steele as her body responded. Thankful the jacket covered her erect nipples, Ivy felt herself getting wet. She tightened her arms around his waist.

"Having fun?" he asked over his shoulder as he reached back with one arm to squeeze her thigh.

"Daddy," she tried to whisper, but the wind whisked that away. Did he know what the vehicle was doing to her?

Ivy rested against him and tried to think of anything else. The scenery flew by, and she admired the flowering trees and green grass decorating the highway. Anything to tune out the continual buzz pressed against her most intimate spot.

Her hands bumped down below his waist when they bounced over a patch on the pavement. Steele controlled the bike perfectly, to her delight. *Oh!*

Her hands were pressing directly on his fly, the buttons bulging slightly as his cock responded to her touch. She had basically groped him without intending to touch him.

"Sorry!" she said loudly so it would reach his ears as she tried to move her hands. He trapped hers in one hand and lifted them back around his waist.

"No tempting Daddy."

By the time they got home, her panties were completely soaked. She hoped when he got up there wouldn't be a wet spot on his seat to betray her arousal. Steele stopped and squeezed her hands to hold her in place.

Twisting to meet her gaze, he instructed, "Be careful of the pipes. Step off and go stand against the house where you'll be safe."

She stepped off, trying to control the shaking of her legs. As she turned to walk to the place he had indicated for her to wait, Ivy saw him scoot back on the seat. He was wiping off the proof of her arousal with his heavy jeans. Ivy felt her face heat and knew she was blushing horribly. *He does know!*

The other Guardians waited for her to be in place before maneuvering their bikes into their normal spots. Steele wrapped an arm around her waist to guide her into the building without saying a word. Discombobulated and trying to look like everything was normal, Ivy relied on him to take care of everything.

When he steered her down the hall to his room, Ivy realized she hadn't thanked the group for coming to escort her home. She paused and turned to go back.

"You can thank them later, Emerald Eyes," Steele assured her.

"Do they know?"

"Yes. Will they ever mention it? No. The club has your back, Little girl. The minute I claimed you for myself, you had their protection."

"But they know," she whispered.

"They're Daddies. They notice more things than others do. Come on, Little girl. Let me take care of you."

Reassured, Ivy nodded and walked with her Daddy to their apartment. Once inside, he scooped her up in his arms and carried her to the bedroom, placing her gently on her feet. His hand cupped the back of her head and pulled her forward to kiss her deeply.

As if that touch turned the key, eliminating the last of her self-control, Ivy grabbed handfuls of his T-shirt and ground herself against his hard frame. When he lifted his lips, she demanded, "I need you now."

"Careful telling Daddy what to do," he warned with a grin that took away any bite his words could carry.

When she bit her bottom lip, Steele smoothed a finger over it. "Only Daddy gets to bite you, Emerald Eyes."

Her "Please!" earned her another kiss. This one seduced and captivated her. How could his kisses rock her world so much?

As she clung to him for stability, Steele efficiently stripped off her dark suit and the professional pumps off her feet. He glanced over her body, clad only in her normal cotton panties and bra. The heat in his eyes made her shiver.

"I'm sorry. I'm not wearing any fancy underwear."

"Little girls don't need to wear anything lacy, sweetheart. I couldn't be any more attracted to you than I am now." He tugged her hand from its grip on his shirt and pressed her palm onto his erection.

She automatically curled her fingers around him to grip him firmly. Staring up into his deep brown eyes, Ivy whispered, "Make it better, Daddy."

In a flash, he had her naked.

"Crawl up on the bed, sweetheart."

She peeked over her shoulder to find his gaze locked on her ass as he unfastened the buttons on his fly. His T-shirt was already gone. Scooting around, she sat on her heels on the mattress, watching the show. After grabbing a condom from the drawer, he shifted onto his hands and knees, and Steele prowled over her, forcing her back on the mattress. He took a minute to help her swing her legs from underneath her before lowering himself to hover over her.

Ivy loved the heat radiating from his body. She ran her hands over his broad chest and down his ribcage to cup his muscular butt. Squeezing the powerful muscles, she watched his face.

"Play all you want, Ivy. I love your touch."

"All I want?" she repeated, raising her eyebrows suggestively.

"You are going to be the death of me," he sighed. His expression completely denied any displeasure with her.

She pushed one of his shoulders, and Steele rolled obediently onto his back. Ivy scrambled after him, straddling his body. As her pussy glided along his thick shaft, Ivy groaned and ground herself on him. Her gaze flew to meet his as Steele captured her hips and held her still.

"Let me protect you, Emerald Eyes."

Boosting her hips up, he quickly opened the small packet and rolled the bright green condom onto his erection.

As she smiled at the color, he told her, "I've gotten rid of all the other colors, Emerald Eyes. I'm fond of this one."

"Daddy. I love you."

"I love you, too, Little girl."

Gripping her waist, Steele drew her down to his body. "Play, Ivy."

With permission given, she squirmed against him as she explored his chest and abdomen. Her eyes closed in delight when he glided his hands up her sides to cup her breasts. Kneading them roughly, he brushed his thumbs over her nipples. She loved the scratch of his work-hardened skin on her body. Steele wasn't a gentleman with manicured, soft hands. He was a Guardian. A welder. A biker.

She leaned forward to press her torso to his and teased him with light kisses until he tangled one hand in her hair and held her in place as his mouth explored hers. He tasted her as if she were the sweetest delight he'd ever sampled. His other hand gripped her bottom with a hold she knew would leave marks tomorrow as he lifted his pelvis to move against hers.

Immediately, her play ended. He was in control. His hand slipped from her tresses to slide between their bodies. His fingers stroked her pink folds to stoke the fire inside her. He tapped lightly on her clit, making her inhale quickly.

"You are so wet, Ivy. Do you want to ride Daddy's cock?"

She nodded. Her body was so ready.

"Good girl."

Steele fitted himself against her slick opening and flexed his hips to enter her. He gripped her ribcage and urged her to sit up, pushing his cock into her completely. "Ride me, Emerald Eyes."

With ferocious desire written on his face, Ivy couldn't feel self-conscious. She bounced experimentally and gasped. His shaft inside her set off so many sensitive spots inside her body. She tried it again and dropped her head back to concentrate on those exquisite sensations.

"Ah!" she gasped at the feel of his fingers pinching her nipples.

"Eyes on me, Little girl. Don't look away."

The intimacy of watching his reactions and seeing the hunger in his eyes pushed her desire higher. She watched him glide a hand over the muscular grooves in his abdomen to stroke her clit. "Come, Little girl. Drench my hand with your wetness."

As if he were in control of her body, Ivy felt the swirling tingles draw together. She screamed into the room as she contracted around his thick cock. She ground herself against him, prolonging the delectable sensations for as long as she could.

"Daddy's turn," Steele announced as he wrapped his arms around her.

Ivy saw the world rotate as he turned their bodies to kneel between her legs.

"Wrap your legs around me, sweetheart."

Fitting her legs around his waist, she locked her feet together at the ankles. As soon as she was in position, Steele lifted his hips and thrust deep inside her. At the end of each stroke, he rubbed his pelvis against her, fueling the sparkles inside her. She bit her lip, trying to resist the growing pleasure.

She held onto him as he plunged into her tight channel. Ivy knew he watched her shifting to create the most sparks inside her. When the feelings were ready to overwhelm her, Steele filled her, revving up his speed. Struggling to stay focused on his face, Ivy saw the moment he lost control. Pure exaltation covered his features, and she felt a rush of warmth as he emptied himself into the condom.

"Come, Ivy!" he shouted into the room as he held her plastered against his body.

With a wordless cry, she succumbed to the delight he treated her to. Grinding her pelvis against him, she fought for every bit of pleasure she could survive.

Minutes later, she lay cuddled against him with her head resting on his shoulder. Her mind still replayed the pleasure she had experienced. Being with Steele was unlike any man she'd ever dated. He made her feel.

Ivy slapped a hand over her tummy when it roared aggressively. Steele let out one of those low chuckles that made her giggle along with him.

"I need to feed you, Little girl. I'm losing my street cred as a Daddy."

"There's street cred for being a Daddy?"

"Only with the Shadowridge Guardians."

She nodded like she knew what went on with the other motorcycle club members. "Think they've eaten everything for dinner?"

"It's taco night. There will be lots."

"Tacos?" She bolted upright and slid off the bed. "Come on. Tacos!"

As he dressed her, Ivy thought about the men in the motorcycle club. She couldn't imagine not knowing the bikers now and felt bad, knowing she thought of them differently now. They had all taught her an important life lesson. While she had always treated everyone respectfully and professionally in her position at the bank, she appreciated these tough, tattooed, and daring Shadowridge Guardians. They protected the community and took care of each other, regardless of what it took. No matter what.

"Thank you for finding me, Daddy."

"I wished I'd caught them at the bank," he said regretfully, pulling on his T-shirt.

"That was the scariest day of my life," Ivy admitted before deciding, "And ultimately, the best day ever."

"Come on, Emerald Eyes. I want to see how many tacos you can eat."

"Six! And you'll eat eight."

"I'll just be warming up at number eight," he teased.

Her giggles filled the hallway as they walked to the kitchen to join everyone.

CHAPTER
TWENTY-ONE

Walking out of her first day of evening classes, she watched the reaction of the other grad students. They hesitated to walk through the mass of tattooed bikers stationed in a group in the parking lot. She moved forward with confidence. Waving at everyone, she wrapped her arms around the handsomest one of all. "Hi, Daddy."

"Hi, Little girl. How did your first day go?"

"Great. They're all scared of you," she whispered.

"I can live with that. Can you?" he asked bluntly, without any sugar coating.

"I won't tell," she promised, smiling up at him.

"Good girl. Ready to go home?"

"Yes, please," she answered politely as she exchanged her book bag for her helmet. She'd decorated it with a sticker bearing the emblem of a rough-looking teddy bear. Ivy was one of them now.

"What are we doing tonight?"

"I'm putting together a set of pipes we have a rush order for. You, my Little grad student, have a lot of homework to do."

"I have all week to finish it," she protested. When he looked at her sternly, she changed her tune. "Okay. I can work on it for a while," she agreed.

"That's my good girl."

Ivy leaned in to whisper in his ear, "Do I get a reward if I finish all my work?"

"Of course, my sweet Emerald Eyes. Let's get you on the bike." Steele brushed away her fingers and fastened the chin strap. As he straddled the bike to hold it steady for her, all the other club members fired up their engines.

Ivy noticed several class members lingering in the area. She knew that she'd have questions to answer the following class session. That was okay. The Shadowridge Guardians had done so much for her, she considered it her personal contribution to the group to give them a hint of professionalism. They didn't need it, of course, but she was determined people should see them as she did. Men who loved hard and protected those they cherished. She couldn't be prouder of her Daddy.

Hugging Steele as they eased into the traffic with the other members of the Guardians, Ivy savored the feel of his hard body against her. When they turned the first right corner, she felt something poke into her leg. Looking down at his saddlebags, Ivy noticed a wooden handle poking out of the secured flap.

When she reached down to touch it at the next stoplight, Steele's hand grasped hers and tugged it back to his waist. Ivy leaned forward to talk.

"What's that, Daddy?"

"A present."

"A present for me?"

"For both of us, actually," he answered as he glided forward, heeding the green light.

Knowing her voice would have to battle the wind now, she waited for the next time they stopped to ask more questions. As they yielded to get on the highway, she took advantage of the chance.

"Who's going to like it better?"

"I can't even hazard a guess, Little girl."

She pondered on that for the entire trip home. How could he not know who would like the gift more? And if it were a present for her, how could it be one for him as well?

By the time they rolled into the Guardians' complex, she was very eager to see what he had brought for them. As always, the men stayed on their bikes until she was safely up by the building. Then they parked their cycles, joking as they always did. She ran back to his side when Steele gave her permission to join him once again.

"Can I see it?" she asked.

"Let's get your helmet off," Steele stated firmly.

Ivy was almost dancing by the time he started to lift the protective device from her head. With a sighed gust of impatience, she ripped it off quickly and then yelped as the buckle got tangled in her hair.

"Little girl," he warned as he carefully freed her without ripping the hair from her scalp.

By the time he finished, they were alone. Steele stowed her helmet with his and finally opened the saddlebag to pull the mysterious present out.

"A paddle?" she asked loudly. Then clapped a hand over her mouth as she looked around to make sure no one had overheard her. *Thank goodness!*

"I think your head feels well enough for you to finally get that spanking I promised you."

"I don't think I need a spanking, Daddy. I've been so good."

Steele just looked at her and held out his hand for hers.

"Can you at least hide it as we walk through crowd inside? They're all going to know," she pleaded.

"Who do you think helped me pick it out?"

"Daddy!" She looked at him, horrified.

Relenting, Steele whisked it behind his back and slid it into the back of his jeans. He extended his hand once again for hers.

With another sigh, Ivy linked her fingers with his. They were all going to know. They'd know anyway. The walls weren't completely soundproofed.

"Come on, Little girl. Let's go enjoy your present. Trust your Daddy."

With each step she took, Ivy felt the zings of arousal gathering inside her. Steele never took control without making sure she enjoyed it. His treatment might be embarrassing, but he always made sure her body loved it.

What would he do this time? The stinging swats he'd landed on her bottom as a warning always made her feel funny inside—like she wanted to feel more. How much more could there be to having a red bottom that hurt to sit on?

His hand squeezed hers, and she looked up to meet his dark eyes. Slowly, she forced her shoulders to relax back into place. She trusted her Daddy with all her heart and mind. He'd saved her from enormous threats to harm her and from the loneliness that had filled her life before.

Ivy tugged her hand from his and latched on to his cut, holding on like she had when he'd first rescued her. His hand folded around hers and he squeezed lightly. He always understood her.

When they got to his apartment, Ivy walked slowly to the bedroom and stood quietly as he undressed her. He said nothing about her damp panties from the ride home and the anticipation of her spanking. When she was completely naked, he ran his hands down her body as his gaze devoured her.

"You are so beautiful, Ivy. I am a very lucky man."

"Daddy," she whispered.

"Yes?" he asked, thinking she wanted to ask a question.

"You're not just a man. You're a lucky Daddy. That's even more special."

"It is, Emerald Eyes. Are you ready?"

"Yes," she said in a wavering voice she couldn't control.

Steele folded a plump pillow in half and placed it on the edge of the bed. Turning, he lifted her and draped her over the cushion on her tummy, presenting her bottom to his view. He stroked over her soft skin.

"Little girls need spankings sometimes to feel—to know who they belong to and who is important in their lives. You are the most precious part of my life, Ivy."

She held her breath and felt the whoosh of air as the paddle moved. Heat filled her senses, and she bit her bottom lip. She couldn't describe that impact with the word sting like his swats. Before she could worry about classifying it, the paddle landed again. Ivy wiggled as a new section of skin warmed. She squeezed her thighs together, feeling her arousal flood from her body.

Repeatedly, he deliberately placed the wooden paddle on her upper thighs and across the rounded curve of her bottom. She wiggled, not trying to evade the tantalizing punishment but in anticipation of where it would land next. Her fingers curled into the soft comforter on the bed for support and to stay in position as he coached her with gentle words that soothed her mind.

When the paddle landed on the bed next to her, she jerked up. He wasn't done, was he? To her delight, he ripped open the nightstand drawer and pulled out a Kelly-green condom. Within seconds, he thrust himself inside her. The feel of his fingers gripping her punished thighs as he held her legs apart and in place added one more layer of sensation. Unable to resist for long, Ivy screamed into the mattress as her body locked around his thick cock, filling her over and over.

"You almost done, Little girl?" Steele asked her two hours later as he cleaned up his tools. He'd skillfully welded the job together that he'd promised to finish that night as she'd worked quietly on the crash bed behind his workspace.

"Yes, Daddy. I just finished the last question."

Ivy shifted carefully on her hot bottom. The lingering effects of his punishment had definitely kept her focused on the tasks she needed to complete for the professor. She'd never admit that to Steele or he'd decide to make it a routine. Or maybe she would, Ivy thought as she slid her laptop back into her bag.

"You're going to have to tell me what that look means," Steele commented.

"Oh, no, Daddy. Bank business. I can't tell you everything."

"We'll see about that. Time for bed, Little girl."

Because of the late hour, he sped her through the shower and into bed with great efficiency. Ivy cuddled on the pillow with Lucky as she watched him turn on her nightlight. She reached back to rub her bottom and felt the cream he'd used to soothe her irritated skin.

"You take good care of me, Daddy," she whispered.

"I try, Little girl. Want to work on cleaning out your house tomorrow?"

"Please. I don't need most of that stuff. I'm happier here with you," she confided in him as he slid into bed and pulled her to his side.

"I'm happier with you here, too, Little girl. Love you."

"I love you, too," she answered before yawning widely.

"Go to sleep, sweetheart."

His lips pressed against her forehead, and she relaxed fully in his arms. Ivy might have named her bear Lucky, but she knew she was even more fortunate.

For some reason, Remi and Carlee popped into her mind. Ivy sent the two other Littles some of her extra luck mentally. They needed to find their Daddies, too.

AUTHOR'S NOTE

I hope you're enjoying the Shadowridge Guardians MC series as much as we are enjoying writing them! The next book in the series is Kade, by Kate Oliver.

Kade: Shadowridge Guardians MC

"Princess, do that again and see what happens…"

Remi is and always has been an MC baby. She's never had a choice in the matter since her dad is a member of the Shadowridge Guardians MC. But she's been avoiding the clubhouse as much as possible the past few years because every time she's near Kade Beckham she can't breathe properly, and she becomes a defensive brat toward him. When she starts getting threatening messages, though, he's the first person she calls for help.

Kade loves his club and takes pride in protecting his brothers. He would do anything for the other members or their family. That's his job after all. Enforcer. So when Remi calls him for help, he doesn't hesitate, but he also knows he needs to keep a wide distance from the prickly little goth girl. But when he finds out her secret, however, he isn't so sure he can stay away. She needs a protector and a Daddy, and he intends to be both.

She can toss that attitude all she wants, but he intends to make her his good girl.

Shadowridge Guardians MC
Steele
Kade
Atlas
Doc
Gabriel
Talon
Bear
Faust
Storm

Combining the sizzling talents of bestselling authors Pepper North, Kate Oliver, and Becca Jameson, the Shadowridge Guardians are guaranteed to give you a thrill and leave you dreaming of your own throbbing motorcycle joyride.

Are you daring enough to ride with a club of rough, growly, commanding men? The protective Daddies of the Shadowridge Guardians Motorcycle Club will stop at nothing to ensure the safety and protection of everything that belongs to them: their Littles, their club, and their town. Throw in some sassy, naughty, mischievous women who won't hesitate to serve their fair share of attitude even in the face of looming danger, and this brand new MC Romance series is ready to ignite!

ALSO BY PEPPER NORTH

Read more from Pepper North

Dr. Richards' Littles®

A beloved age play series that features Littles who find their forever Daddies and Mommies. Dr. Richards guides and supports their efforts to keep their Littles happy and healthy.

Available on Amazon

Dr. Richards' Littles®

is a registered trademark of

With A Wink Publishing, LLC.

All rights reserved.

SANCTUM

Pepper North introduces you to an age play community that is isolated from the surrounding world. Here Littles can be Little, and Daddies can care for their Littles and keep them protected from the outside world.

Available on Amazon

Soldier Daddies

What private mission are these elite soldiers undertaking? They're all searching fShadowridge Guardians MCgirl.

Available on Amazon

The Keepers

This series from Pepper North is a twist on contemporary age play romances. Here are the stories of humans cared for by specially selected Keepers of an alien race. These are science fiction novels that age play readers will love!

Available on Amazon

The Magic of Twelve

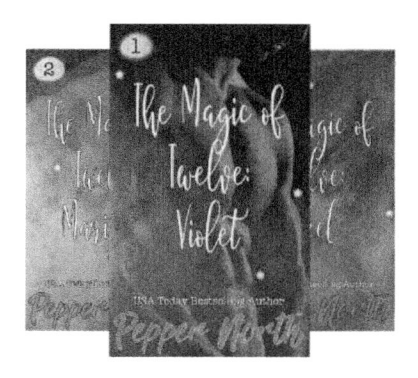

The Magic of Twelve features the stories of twelve women transported on their 22nd birthday to a new life as the droblin (cherished Little one) of a Sorcerer of Bairn. These magic wielders have waited a long time to take complete care of their droblin's needs. They will protect their precious one to their last drop of magic from a growing menace. Each novel is a complete story.

Available on Amazon

ABOUT THE AUTHOR

Ever just gone for it? That's what *USA Today* Bestselling Author Pepper North did in 2017 when she posted a book for sale on Amazon without telling anyone. Thanks to her amazing fans, the support of the writing community, Mr. North, and a killer schedule, she has now written more than 80 books!
Enjoy contemporary, paranormal, dark, and erotic romances that are both sweet and steamy? Pepper will convert you into one of her loyal readers. What's coming in the future? A Daddypalooza!

Sign up for Pepper North's newsletter

Like Pepper North on Facebook

Join Pepper's Readers' Group for insider information and giveaways!

Follow Pepper everywhere!
Amazon Author Page
BookBub

FaceBook
GoodReads
Instagram
TikToc
Twitter
YouTube
Visit Pepper's website for a current checklist of books!

Don't miss future sweet and steamy Daddy stories by Pepper North? Subscribe to my newsletter!

Printed in Great Britain
by Amazon